Home Is a Lot More Than Just a Place to Hang Your Hat

Larry Webb

PublishAmerica
Baltimore

ISBN: 1-60672-840-7
PUBLISHED BY PUBLISHAMERICA, LLLP
www.publishamerica.com
Baltimore

Printed in the United States of America

Doctor Dole

Be sure to read and
enjoy. The really good
guy in here is the "Doc".
Let me know what you
think.

Love,

Larryw133@comcast.net

Chapter One

I remember the weekend I decided to run away. It started out pleasantly enough when Mom said I could go to the movies to celebrate my report card. Like always, I rode my bike to the theater locking it up in the bike rack at the side of the building. The movie was great, the popcorn was ok, and my friends were rowdy. So what's new? When it was over I jumped on my bike and rode home. I pretty much stayed to the main streets and didn't take any shortcuts as my parents were a little nervous about my being out this late and riding through town all by myself. They always wanted me to keep to the most populated and best lit stretches. I thought they were a little over protective, but at least I got to do some things—sometimes. After all, I was eleven years old and should have some freedoms.

Doing a wheelie and then skidding to a stop, I dumped my bike by the back door and slipped in, hopefully un-noticed because it was close to midnight which was a bit late even for Friday night standards. Oh well, I was celebrating with Mom's permission so it was really ok. There was a light on in the living room—not a good sign. Dad was waiting up for me. My only hope was that he would be sober. Fat chance of that! It was Friday night and he was soused every Friday night. What really added to our family merriment was the fact that Dad was a mean drunk. Therefore, no buddy overnights on a weekend—ever!

Stumbling across the kitchen floor he roared at the top of his lungs as he smacked me with the back of his hand knocking me to the floor. I had thrown up my arms to ward off the blow and lost my balance and landed in a heap. Strange how he never left any bruises that could be readily seen by the general public—like my teachers.

"Where have you been?" he snarled in his ugliest voice. "Out with those weird friends of yours again? You're supposed to be in the house no later than ten o'clock! You're either the stupidest kid I've ever met or the most bull headed!"

He lit into me with his belt not even pretending to wait for an answer. I rolled across the floor covering up the best I could as he beat the devil out of me.

When he finally stopped, he was gasping for breath as he spit out, "Get to bed, you worthless little piece of crap!"

He gasped for breath, coughed a few times, and waddled back to his beer. At five foot, nine inches tall and two hundred and fifty pounds, he was downright fat and out of shape. Mr. America, he wasn't. Mr. Bully, he was.

I slipped out of my room the next morning as all appeared quiet and headed for the kitchen. I was going to grab a bowl of cereal and get out of there. I didn't want to face him or listen to his lies and self pity. Last night's episode had happened just once too often. It was always the same. He'd get drunk, beat up on me, and then be all apologies the next morning. I don't know how many times I heard about how sorry he was and how he didn't know what he was doing and how he was going to quit drinking. As I saw it, it was all a line of bull. He liked getting drunk, and he got his kicks out of knocking me around.

"Jason, come here," he called from the living room.

Here we go again, I thought. Same story, 875th verse. How many times has this scene replayed itself?

"Son, I'm really sorry about last night. Mom told me that you were going to be late, and I guess I forgot or it didn't' register or something."

"Yeah, sure, Dad. Forget it. It just happened. No big deal." Right! We'll forget the whole thing, that is until next weekend when we do it all again—that is unless I'm real lucky and he manages to get himself drunked up on his Wednesday bowling night. Then we can jump start the weekend festivities.

"At-a-boy, Jason. That's the attitude. Live and let live, forgive and forget. That's my boy!" He laughed as he mussed up my hair with his hands. I hated it when he messed up my hair. Every time it was the same phony crap. He could spout it out faster than anyone, and he never meant one word of it.

"Oh, by the way! That was a great report card again. Four A's and two B's? Good thing you inherited your mother's brains kid. You just keep it up. You're doing great!"

That was the end of the discussion. Just say you're sorry, joke around a little bit, muss up the kid's hair, and it's all over and forgotten. You bet! Mom and dad never intended to have kids. I was an accident and they both let me know it on several occasions. I cramped their style.

I headed back to the kitchen and my cereal and Dad followed. "We need to discuss something that has come up. Mom and I have been meaning to tell you for some time, but we just haven't found the right time to do it. Anyway, I've accepted a new position in a law firm in Michigan so we are going to move to the capitol city, Lansing. We are actually going to be leaving Monday. Yesterday was my last day of work at the law office here. Just think! We're going to get out of all this heat and humidity and move to a place that is a little cooler in the summer. Isn't that great? You're going to have to go through all your stuff this week end and pack for the move. It's a great time to get rid of all the junk you have lying around that you never use any more."

"Dad! We've only been here six months, and you promised that this would be our last move. You said we would be able to stay here, settle down, and make permanent friends."

"I know, but this job came up in a big law firm up there. When I heard about it six months ago, I contacted them, took the Michigan Bar Exam, and one thing led to another. Do you remember when I went up there for a few days on business? Well, that's what the business was. This move is worth a lot of money to us. We'll have a bigger house, more influential friends, and life will be great for all of us."

"Dad, I don't want to move! I'm just now starting to make friends again. Don't you realize how hard it is for me to be moving all the time, or don't you care?"

"Don't be a smart mouth or you're apt to get smacked again. We have to go where the best opportunities are for me and your mom. It's a bigger law firm than the one here in St. Pete, and like I said, a lot more money. You'll just have to adjust."

Yeah, sure! I'd have to adjust. Every time I settled into a new school, I had to start all over again. I was in the seventh grade and had been in five different schools. Each move meant a new town, a new house, a new school, a new bunch of teachers, and all new friends. At least I managed to keep my head screwed on straight, keep my grades up, and make enough friends so I didn't' go crazy.

"So, when did you say we were going to make this move?" I asked being careful of my tone. If Dad thought I was being mouthy, he'd blast me.

"The moving van will be here Monday—two days from now.

They load up our stuff and then we all head out of town. We'll drive on ahead of them and probably stay in a motel for a day or so until they get there and get us unloaded. It'll be an adventure."

"Monday morning!" I choked. "We can't leave Monday! I have a presentation to give in social studies on Wednesday. I didn't said goodbye to my friends. I didn't even check out of school. I can't just disappear!"

"Well, I guess that's just too bad for you. Like I said earlier, we intended to tell you about it sooner, but we were busy and never got around to it. Besides, what difference does it make to you anyway? You're just a kid. You'll be okay."

Right! I may have been just a kid, but I had feelings too. He didn't realize it, but my friends and school were just as important to me as his, probably more so because he didn't have that many friends.

I decided right then and there that I was not going. I wandered out into the yard and called my buddy, Chris Jackson. He was the first kid I met in St. Petersburg, and we had been best of friends since.

"Chris, Jason here. What are you doing?"

"Watching Tiger Woods kill the competition on TV. Why, what's up?"

"I want to talk to you privately. Can I come over?"

"Sure, we can always go into the den and pretend we're watching this silly thing. Nobody will bother us there. Mom's busy making cookies and Dad's at the hospital making rounds."

Chris's dad was a doctor. Seems like everyone in our subdivision was a doctor, lawyer, Indian chief, or professional of some kind. There was a lot of money around us, but that sure didn't seem to make people real happy. Lots of my friends had split families—divorces and all that.

Obviously, I wasn't the only with problems around there.

Chris wasn't very happy with his home life either. His dad was never home, and I mean never. He couldn't even come home for dinner but what there would be an emergency situation of some kind at the hospital with one of his patients, and he'd get called in. I don't see how his mom could stand it. I know Chris couldn't. He had a good relationship with his dad and resented the time the hospital and his practice kept him from home. They couldn't even toss the football around without his cell phone jangling away.

My dad was around a lot, and I couldn't stand that. He was totally frustrated professionally, but he didn't think there was anything else he could do. He spent years in college and figured he was locked into his profession as a result. He had changed law firms six or seven times that I could remember. He hated the job so much it affected his relationships with his bosses and clients. Therefore, one year was about the maximum he'd stay in one place. Either he would get mad and quit, or they would ask him to look elsewhere. I felt sorry for him because he was so miserable. However, I didn't like the way he took it out on me. He never raised his voice to my mom, yet he'd backhand me for walking too heavily across the carpet. Mom never said a word to him about it either. She knew what he was doing was wrong. Actually, I think she was afraid of him. It was easier for her to have him take his frustrations out on me than her.

Chapter Two

I slid into Chris's driveway and dumped my bike on the side of the drive where it would be safe. He was watching out the window and met me the door. "Come one in, Jason. I was just getting ready to raid those warm cookies, so you might as well give me a hand."

"Sounds good to me," I said. "Got any milk to go with them?"

We headed into the den where the golf match was still going on. About as exciting as watching paint dry. Chris hauled in a bowl full of cookies and a gallon of milk. We were all set so I started to unload my troubles on Chris.

"You know what jerks I live with, well, the old man told me about an hour ago that we are moving to Michigan on Monday. Seems that they forgot to tell me."

"You're moving? Monday? Boy, they sure gave you a lot of advanced notice, didn't they? What kind of a deal is that?"

"Crappy as always. I'm not going either. I'm running away. Want to help me?"

"Sure, what do you want me to do?"

"I really don't know, Chris. The only thing I know for sure is that I'm not going with them. I've had it. All we've ever done is move, move, move…and this time I'm not going to. I'm staying here in St. Pete if I have to live out of a box along with the homeless dudes under the overpass."

"How long do you think we could hide you out before someone discovers you?"

"I don't know, but I'll bet I can stay out of sight until after they leave Monday. They sure won't hold up this 'Golden Opportunity du jour' just because I decided to split. They'll probably figure good riddance."

Chris and I hashed out all kinds of different scenarios and finally decided I would hide out at his house until after they left on Monday and then we'd kind of play it by ear after that. He could sneak me food behind his parent's backs, and they would never become the wiser. My parents would have no clue where I was. They knew Chris by sight because he would come by the house to get me on occasion, but we never hung out there so they really didn't know him at all. They could care less about my friends so they didn't know his last name much less where he lived. All my friends were creeps and weirdoes according to them.

Chris's bedroom was at the end of a hallway on the main level of the house with a door leading to the side yard practically beside his bedroom door. I could sneak in and out unnoticed by his parents. His mom and dad rarely went to his room, and if they did, they knocked. They respected his privacy. The only problem might be the cleaning lady. She came on Mondays, but as long as I was out of there by 10 in the morning, no sweat! I would have to stay out of sight for a couple of hours because she was normally there until noon. Chris was a slob so we always joked that it took her more time to clean his room than the rest of the house together. There were socks and underwear lying around all over the place.

Sunday afternoon finally arrived and the old folks cooperated by going out to dinner with his ex boss so they could clear up some last minute details of his leaving. Hopefully they'd be gone for hours. Naturally, Dad would be drunk when he got home so Mom would immediately disappear to her bedroom and read while Dad would start thinking about what kind of trouble I might have gotten myself into while they were gone. Anything for an excuse. Of course, if he couldn't figure out anything I might have done, he could just beat the tar out of me on general principles. He'd either do that or pass out on the sofa in the living room. Exciting life I led.

Mom was her usual thoughtful self. She left a can of tomato soup on the counter with a can of tuna so I could gorge myself on a couple of tuna fish sandwiches while they were suffering through their prime rib and lobster.

As soon as I finished my gourmet meal, I went to the closet and dug out my sleeping bag. I stuffed clean underwear, socks, and three or four changes of clothes in the bottom of it, rolled it up, and headed for Chris's. I shot him a quick text message so he'd have the door unlocked and ready for me when I got there. I figured I was ready for a short while anyway—at least until after Monday. Had no idea what would happen then. Hadn't thought that far in advance. I only knew that I had to hide out until they left.

Chris met me in the back yard when I got there. "The coast is clear, "he said. "Mom's at some deaconess meeting at church, and dad's at the hospital. Hide your bike in the shed and nobody will see it. Then bring your stuff in."

We stashed my sleeping bag under his bed and headed for the kitchen to raid the frig. Theirs was always more interesting to check out than ours. Mrs. Jackson liked to cook so there were always a bunch of leftovers sitting in there just waiting for us to munch on.

Dinner at the Jackson's was always lots of fun—especially if Doc was there. Mrs. J always put dinner on the table at exactly 7 PM regardless of who was there. I never horned in on a meal that didn't take at least an hour. Doc pumped everybody for information. What was going on at school? What did you think about who was running for governor? Did we watch the last space flight lift off? Why not? What did our progress reports look like? What did our report cards look like? Doc and Mrs. J knew more about me than my parents did. The funny part was, they acted like they really cared.

At our house we ate around Dad's whims and schedule. Therefore, I never knew when we were going to eat. It could be anywhere between four-thirty and eight. Naturally, it was my job to psyche out the schedule of the day and be there to eat on time. If I came in late, I wasn't allowed to eat. One time I came home right at five o'clock just as they were finishing dinner. Dad grabbed the leftover meat loaf and three baked potatoes and ran them down the garbage disposal. They'd teach be to be responsible if it killed all of us. Fat chance of that happening.

If he had to leave for a meeting, Mom would usually make sure I got something to eat. If not, I would manage to get myself over to the Jacksons. If I could get there before seven thirty or so, I would get fed. Mrs. J never bought the story that I wasn't hungry and didn't really come over there for dinner. Chris clued them in regularly on my situation. They never mentioned it, but they looked out for me.

Anyway, with Chris's parents gone for the afternoon, I figured we would be pretty safe just hanging around playing computer games. Chris thought otherwise. "Jason, we've got to hide out somewhere and then come back here late tonight. Otherwise, your parents might just figure out where you are and come here looking. I'll leave a note for Mom telling her that I'm going to the movies and will be late. Then we can ride over to the beach and hang out there for the day."

"The beach? Chris, it's cold over there! No one but the Snowbirds goes to the beach on the first week of November."

"Your point? That's just about the last place anyone would look for us."

We grabbed out bikes and peddled over to St. Petersburg Beach which was just a couple of miles away. We spent most of the day at a closed up snack bar beyond the pink hotel. We decided we'd have to play the next week by ear. There was no way I could go to school because that's the first place my dad, the police, or whoever would look. Chris would have to carry on as usual, and I would go into hiding. That way no one would guess that we were together.

On the way home that evening we separated right after we left the beach. He took the main route past the theater and headed home taking the most direct and obvious path just in case anyone was watching. I took the scenic route sneaking in the back way cutting through the back yards there in his neighborhood. I hid my bike in the bushes behind their garage and then sneaked in the back door that we had left unlocked.

It took Chris about a half hour before he could get away from his mom and head for his bedroom claiming he was really tired and wanted to go to bed. She didn't really buy this "movie" story and was asking a lot of pointed questions which forced him to lie like a bandit. When he opened the door I was inconspicuously hiding in his bathtub behind the shower curtain.

"So what's going on?" I whispered after he moseyed in and shut the door.

"The police are looking for you. Your dad searched your room when they couldn't find you and discovered a bunch of your clothes gone. I guess they kind of figured it out. "

"What did you tell your mom?"

"Nothing really. She pretends to believe everything I say and sometimes just doesn't force me into lying. I told her I went down to the movies by myself and didn't know exactly where you were, which wasn't really a lie. I rode my bike past the theater on the way home, and I didn't know for sure if you had come in the back door yet, if you were hiding under the bed again, or what."

"So what did the cops say?"

"Just that you had taken off because you didn't want to move, and they figured we were together some place. They have you listed as a run-away, and I'm a 'Person of interest' whatever that means."

"How the heck did they get that all figured out? Dad might know you by sight and for sure doesn't know your last name. I'm not all that sure that he even knows your first name. As far as he's concerned you're just another low life like me."

"That may be true, but your mom knows me by name. She's the one who tipped them off."

"Look, if I can keep out of sight until after tomorrow, I'll be home free. The moving van is due at nine, and it should be loaded by sometime in the early afternoon and then they'll head out. When that thing pulls out of the drive, my parents will be following right behind."

"Jason, use your head. You don't think for a minute that they'd just pull out and follow the van and leave you behind, do you?"

"Sure they would. He'll just leave it to the police to find me and send me to Michigan when and if they do. Chris, face it. He doesn't like me and never has. He'd be just fine with having me out of his hair."

"I don't think so. He may not be the world's greatest father, but he isn't going to just pull up stakes and leave you here while he heads out for Michigan. Your mom might have a little to say about that one."

"No she won't. He'll convince her that the police will find me and scare me to death before sending me on to them. He'll give her all the lawyer BS about how they'll put me in a juvie home for a few days while they are contacting them and it will do me good. And she'll buy into it. Anything not to shake the bushes and get him mad at her. She'll go along with anything just to keep the peace. In the meantime, what say we get some sleep? Tomorrow will take care of itself."

I spread out on my sleeping bag right beside Chris's bed and against the wall and on the opposite side from the door. In case of an emergency, like someone coming in, I could pull myself under his bed. I didn't think I'd be able to get to sleep because of all the excitement of the day, but that was no problem. My eyelids almost woke me up when they slammed shut.

Sometime later there was a loud knock on the door. "Chris, wake up! I'm coming in to talk to you." Oh, oh! Doc was home and he didn't sound too happy.

I was fired up mentally with the first bang on the door. I grabbed the springs under his mattress and pulled myself under the bed sleeping bag and all.

What a difference! My dad would have just barged in yelling. I didn't have a whole lot of privacy.

Chris stuck his head over the side and whispered, "You all set?"

"Yeah, go ahead, "I answered. "Let him in."

"Da...Dad? Is that you?" Chris mumbled almost incoherently. What an acting job!

Dr. Jackson walked in and turned on the light beside the bed. "Chris," he said. "We need to talk."

"Wha...what time is it?" Chris yawned as he sat up rubbing his eyes.

17

"I know, it's late, and I'm sorry, Dr. Jackson said as he sat down on the side of the bed. "It's a little past midnight, but I just got home from the hospital. Where is Jason?"

He sure didn't' waste any time getting to the point.

"Jason? Jason who?" Chris asked kind of stupidly. He still wasn't completely awake yet.

"Chris, can the act! Mr. Anderson called me at the hospital, and he was livid. I can't really say that I blame him. They are planning to head north tomorrow and Jason has run off. I find it very hard to believe that you don't know where he is. You need to tell me what is going on and where he is. Now!"

"Don't even ask, Dad. Don't force me to lie to you. Mr. Anderson is about the meanest, most abusive person I've ever heard of. He's always beating up on Jason for no reason except for the fact that he's drunk, and now he's pulled this stunt. Jason said that he's not going, and I don't blame him. Dad, Mr. Anderson just told him yesterday that they were moving."

"Chris, that isn't the point. Jason isn't doing the right thing either by running away. That never solved anything. And, if you're helping him, you're in the wrong too. The Andersons have to work out their own problems, and you just can't get involved. I'm sure, he's just disappointed about the move, and that's all there really is to it.

"No, it isn't! I've seen the bruises on him, and they aren't from disappointment. Mr. Anderson is a drunk who hates his job and his kid and takes out his frustrations on Jason."

"I think you're exaggerating a bit here, and besides, it's not very gentlemanly to call someone a drunk especially when you don't know all the facts."

"Dad, I do know the facts this time, and what I told you is the truth. I'm not telling where Jason is hiding out. His parents can just go off without him. They've made no bones about the fact that they don't want him. His dad actually told him that he wasn't his and that he was a mistake from the beginning. He shouldn't have ever been. How would you like to grow up with that?"

"That would be tough to hear, but the fact remains that they are not just going to head out and leave him here. People just don't do that so what you are doing is just making it worse.

Listen, I like Jason. He seems like a really nice kid, but the reality is you just don't know what goes on behind closed doors in a person's home. If he isn't exaggerating, and his dad is abusing him, that can be handled by the authorities. Running away isn't solving anything. Running away is always a poor decision."

"But, Dad, that's where you're wrong. You could do something about it. You're a doctor. You know all kinds of important people. You could do something for him if you wanted to."

"The courts don't act on hearsay. I couldn't any more go to the authorities and cry child abuse without any proof than I could fly."

"You've done it before. You've turned people in to the authorities."

"True, but those kids who had been brought in with injuries of one kind or the other, and I personally saw the welts and bruises as I took care of their broken arms, legs, or whatever. Stuff like that is reason for suspicion and can be reported to Child Protective Services."

"So what you're saying is that Jason has to become an emergency room case or worse before anything can be done. In the meantime, it's just fine if he gets his butt beat two or three times a week just as long as he doesn't end up in the hospital or morgue."

That was just great. Chris and Dr. Jackson were arguing over me, and I was hiding under the bed. I should have just slid out from under the bed and let Dr. Jackson call my dad or the police to stop their arguing, but I didn't.

I expected to hear Dr. Jackson start smacking Chris around every time he opened his mouth, but he didn't. My dad would have knocked me silly long ago the way he was talking. About a half hour after he came in, Doc got up to leave. "Remember one thing. You told me not to make you lie when I first came in. I tried very hard not to. I'll even give you credit for telling me that you wouldn't tell where Jason is instead of lying by saying you didn't know. However, you and Jason need to spend some time tomorrow morning and talk over what you and I discussed tonight. Both of you have some responsibility in this. You both need to make good choices and do the right thing, and I am trying to provide you some time to do it that way. That's why I'm not looking in the closet or under your bed, which would probably result in my warming a couple of bottoms and calling the authorities tonight. In the meantime, you both need to get some sleep. No one will disturb you for the rest of the night so Jason would probably sleep better on the bed than under it or tucked away in the walk in closet. Oh, by the way. I put Jason's bike in the garage so it wouldn't be left out all night and maybe be seen by the wrong people."

As soon as he walked out the door and closed it, I squirmed my way from under the bed. "He knows!" we both whispered wide eyed at the same time.

"Now what?" I asked.

"Get up here in the bed where we can talk. So, how'd I do?" Chris asked as I slid under the covers.

"Great!" I answered. I just don't know how you got away with it. My dad would have beat the living crap out of me two minutes into that discussion."

"Not my dad. I don't remember the last time he hit me. He has never been mean to me unless I really deserved it. Then, it was always been on the seat of the pants with his hand. He'd rather talk and try to make me understand his point of view and make me feel ashamed—just like he was doing tonight. He's always been able to put me on a real guilt trip. You couldn't see him but he grinned when he mentioned warming a couple of bottoms tonight. I really don't think he would have, however...."

"I guess some people are just born lucky and others are like me. Pity party time! Anyway, what are we going to do now? I can't stay here or we'll get caught. Now we both know that if your dad actually catches me here, he'll turn me in to the authorities. He won't be forced into lying either."

"I don't know," Chris said. "Maybe we should go down to the beach and hide out for a few days and figure out what we're going to do. We can always mooch food and money off the tourists."

"You mean you'd be willing to go along with me?"

"Sure! I think you're doing the right thing, and I'm going to stick with you until we get this thing straightened out."

"That's great, Chris. Now, if we just had enough money to tide us over for a few days, we might be able to swing it. I'd hate to try it broke though. I grabbed everything I had lying around this morning, but that only came to about eighteen dollars."

"Then we'll be okay for a little while. I've got about twenty-five dollars in my drawer, so let's do it. We don't have to stay gone long, just long enough for your parents to give up and leave town without you. Then we can come back here. I'm sure my parents could be talked into letting you stay once they understand the whole situation. Besides, they'll be so glad to have me back by then they'll probably go along with anything. In the meantime, let's try to go to sleep. It's really late."

21

Chapter Three

Knowing that we had enough money to last a few days settled it. We slept like logs until morning. When his alarm went off for school, he got up as usual, showered, and headed to the kitchen for breakfast. Doc had already left and his mom was leaving to work at the food bank where she volunteered every Monday. Perfect! As soon as she left, Chris yelled out that the coast was clear. I jumped in the shower and then came out for breakfast.

Chris was smiling when I got out there. "Mom told me I looked a little peaked this morning so if I wanted to stay home from school, it was okay. They are both in on this." While I ate breakfast he wrote a long note to his parents explaining everything. He told them that we both had our cell phones so in case of an emergency one of us would call. He also told them that we turned off our cells so not to call us because we wouldn't get the message. We both laughed when thinking about the voice messages that they would leave.

After breakfast we headed out on our bikes. After getting out of the neighborhood, we did a little detour and headed for St. Pete's Beach. Normally it took us a little over an hour to get there from my house, but we decided to take the scenic route so we wouldn't run into any policemen on the way. That took longer. Once we were in the area, we would blend in with all the tourists.

We arrived at the pier close to noon which was a huge tourist trap because of the upside down pyramid at the end of the dock filled with restaurants, bars, knick knack shops, and more. We both had to make a quick trip to the bathroom so we headed for the public restroom. Coming out of there we spied a peddler hawking hot dogs for an outrageous price. We both bought a couple apiece along with a drink. It didn't' take a couple of geniuses to figure that our money wasn't going to last forever eating extravagantly like that. We had to supplement our cash.

With all the people milling around it was safe to pedal across the causeway to the beach. Nobody would pay any attention to a couple of eleven year olds in that area, so we hopped on our bikes and were on our way.

Once we were on the beach we had to stash the bikes. We started looking for some kind of abandoned house or winter home where the snowbirds hadn't arrived yet. That was pretty tough, but we finally found a place. We locked up our bikes behind their garage to a pole with a basketball hoop on it— hoping they would be there when we came back. Chris wrote down the address and put it in his pocket along with a little hand drawn map so we could find our way back.

Once we got to the water's edge the temperature was only seventy degrees, but the sun was shining brightly. We couldn't imagine ourselves in the water that day. I think we would have frozen. No self respecting Floridian would be caught swimming in the ocean in November.

You sure couldn't tell it was winter just by looking around. All kinds of Yankees spread out on blankets soaking up the sun. I wondered if anyone from the North ever worked or went to school. Most of them had to be in Florida most of the time. Of course, I can't say as if I blamed them. If the Northern winters and ice and snow are as bad as the transplants at school said it was, I'd want to come down to the beach too.

We spotted two girls about our age sitting on a blanket looking out over the water. "What are you looking at?" I asked as we stopped in front of them striking up a conversation.

"The answer is for, not at," the blond answered with a smile. "Everyone told us about all the porpoise around here, and we haven't seen one yet."

"It's the wrong time of day," Chris answered. "You want to be here about six in the morning or about dusk. During the day it's a waste of time looking for them because they aren't feeding."

"Well, I guess that takes care of that!" she said disgustedly as she headed for the water. "I'm going swimming."

"Me too," her friend replied as she got up to follow. Looking back over her shoulder, she called back to us, "How come you two don't have on your suits?"

"It's too darned cold for that. Besides, we Floridians normally just go skinny dipping when we take the notion to go in the water," I called back to her with a straight face. "If you want to wait a minute though, we'll strip down and join you in the water."

"Oh, that's ok," one of them yelled back. We could see her blush from there. "I guess we'll just swim by ourselves."

All four of us laughed and waved goodbye to each other as Chris and I headed down the beach. About a hundred yards and five-hundred people later Chris turned to me smiling, "Now that could have been a rather profitable bull session."

"Why?" I asked. "What do you mean?"

"One of them had three ten dollar bills tucked into her shoe. I saw them when we first stopped, but didn't think that much more about them until they up and headed for the water. They were easy picking. When you spread that line about skinny dipping, I sat down pretending to start taking off my shoes, and slipped one of them out of her shoe."

"Why did you only take one?"

"I figured that when they come back to shore, if they happened to check their money, they would see the wad in the shoe and hopefully wouldn't bother counting. If they did count it, maybe they'd just think one of the tens blew out or something. They probably wouldn't suspect someone actually stole from them because a thief would have taken all of it. Anyway, it doesn't matter 'cause then I couldn't do it so I put it back."

"Good. I wasn't real comfortable with the idea of stealing, even if we did say we would have to supplement our money one way or the other. I just kind of thought that maybe we could run errands for tips or something. "

So we did. We spent the rest of the day helping old people carry their blankets and belongings back to their cars. Worked out rather profitably too.

When the sun started to go down, it cooled off fast. We couldn't stay on the beach because that steady breeze off the Gulf was cold. We had to find a place to spend the night.

"Let's go back and check the bikes," Chris said. "We can always sleep in that garage if nobody is around."

It took us a while to get back because we stopped off at a little café and blew some of our day's profits on a couple more hot dogs.

The first thing we did was check out the surroundings when we got back. Nobody had touched our bikes and the house was empty and pretty isolated. It was as good a place to crash for the night as any. We hadn't noticed earlier, but the garage door had a padlock on it. There was a window around in back where we had the bikes stashed so we checked that out. Ta Da! It was unlocked.

"Here we go," I whispered to Chris. "Just what the doctor ordered."

I crawled through the window first and Chris followed. Man, it was dark in there! We should have checked the place out earlier while it was still light enough to see. As it was, about all we could do was sit with our backs against the wall and try to stay as warm as possible until the sun came up again. That place creaked and squeaked all night long. I'm sure I didn't get a wink of sleep and I nearly froze to death.

Wouldn't you know it! When daylight finally came not five feet from where we sat shivering all night was a stack of old blankets and a Coleman lantern.

"Would you look at this?" Chris moaned when we spotted them. "And I froze my butt off all night long."

"Yeah, me too, "I groaned. "Oh well, at least we know what's in here now. Today we'll have to grab some matches someplace 'cause this lantern is full."

"In the meantime, I'm starved!" Chris grumbled. "I wonder what Mom is fixing for breakfast this morning. It's too bad we can't sneak back there for a hot shower and breakfast before we head out for the day again."

"Hey, Chris! You aren't getting homesick on me all ready are you? We just left yesterday."

"No, I'm just hungry, tired, and grouchy. Let's head back to the beach and see what we can find to eat."

"Okay, but no hotdogs today. My stomach is about half screwed up after all of them we ate yesterday."

"Agreed. I don't feel so hot either. Probably a good idea to keep an eye on the public johns today." Chris grinned.

Oatmeal and toast actually tasted pretty good even though I wouldn't ever admit it in public. After we finished we slipped off the stools in the greasy spoon and headed out.

We were turning into first class snoops so we decided to check out the dumpster behind the Holiday Inn. We were so engrossed in what we were doing, we didn't hear footsteps coming behind us. "Boys, I'd like a word with you," came a rather ominous voice behind us.

We almost wet our pants right on the spot. It was a St. Pete's Beach cop. Without a word, we both split as if by reflex. Chris went right and I went left. I don't know where the cop went. All I know is that I didn't stop running until I reached that old refreshment stand nearly three miles away. I sat on one of the old cement stools and gasped for air. Fifteen minutes later my heart settled down to about two-hundred and ten beats a minute, and I was getting enough oxygen to start thinking again.

I had no idea what to do next. If that cop caught Chris, it was all over for him, but not for me. I thought he might actually want to get caught so he could go home anyway. It would be an easy out for him. I just hoped he'd keep his mouth shut about where we were hiding out and not go back for his bike for a day or so. By that time I'd be long gone.

Decision time. I'd just stay put for a while and see what happened. It was cold out there at the refreshment stand with the Gulf breeze blowing in, so I lay down behind the retaining wall out of the wind and tried to stay warm. It was nice an cozy. Without even realizing it, I drifted off to sleep.

I must have dozed off for a couple of hours because when I woke up, the sun was high in the sky and there were all kinds of people around. The hunger pangs were gnawing again too. It had been a long time since breakfast and I was starved.

Chris and I pretty much split all of our money in half along with the tips we earned helping old people carry their stuff. After all of our hotdogs yesterday and breakfast this morning, I still had a touch over twenty dollars. To heck with it, I thought. I decide to splurge and buy a real live lunch. I left the beach and headed for the street. There were literally dozens of restaurants in all price ranges to choose from.

Finally, I spotted the exact sign that I had been looking for. The café advertised a luncheon special of a hamburger, fries, and a small shake for $4.99. They even had a bathroom. It was my lucky day. I went into the restaurant and headed immediately for the john. Much relieved I came out, found a stool, and sat down.

My waitress turned out to be one of those delights you would always dream of taking home to introduce to your parents one day.

"Yeah, Kid. What'll you have?" she asked cracking her gum as she talked. What a charmer. Her once-upon-a-time bleached blonde hair was at least half brown from the roots out. It looked like she had just walked a mile down the beach and hadn't bothered to brush it out. Her outfit had gravy and food splotched all over it. Um, yummy!

"I'll take the luncheon special, "I smiled not able to stop gawking at the mess.

"Want anything to drink?" she cracked and snapped and blowing a tiny bubble.

"Doesn't the special come with a shake?"

"Yeah, but you don't get water unless you ask for it. The ice machine is broke so it won't be real cold."

"I would like a glass of water, please."

That "please" got to her, I think. I don't imagine she heard that word around there all that often.

It was funny watching her because it was obvious she hated her job. She stomped up and down behind the counter pouring coffee for those who waved their cups at her and never actually exchanged a pleasantry with anyone.

Her jaws never stopped crushing that gum either as she paced back and forth like a feral cat. "Here you go, Kid," was the closest thing to a friendly remark she came as she tossed my lunch down in front of me. She actually reminded me of my dad. I'll bet she enjoyed making herself and everyone around her miserable.

If nothing else, she made me more determined than ever that I was not going home again even if I were alone now. I began wondering if I could find another run-away to team up with. I had no idea where Chris was. Besides, he was showing signs of being homesick. If he did happen to get away from that cop, he might have had enough of this by now anyway and called his parents to come and get him. I probably should have turned on my cell, but I really didn't want to hear any of my messages from anyone.

"That'll be $5.39 with the tax, Kid. Are you done with that plate?"

"One more thing, "I said. "Could I have a pack of gum? I don't care what kind it is as long as it's sugarless. Surprise me."

The gum was a real spur of the moment thing that I couldn't afford, but couldn't resist. After she bought back my change, I waited until she was busy at the far end of the counter. Then I slipped a piece of that sugarless gum under my napkin for her tip—sweet thing that she was—and headed for the door. I know it was gutless, but I wanted to be out of there when she found it. I doubt seriously if she would ever see the connection between her personality and the gum, and I really didn't care.

I passed the rest of the day just walking around. I must have traveled the entire length of the beach and back a couple of times. As dusk was starting to show on the horizon, I headed back to the garage. On the way I slipped into another restaurant and bar combo and grabbed a pack of matches. At least I could light the lantern at the garage and have a little light and warmth.

When I arrived there was a blanket over the window. I didn't know what to do. Was Chris in there or someone else? Had the people come home and noticed the open window and decided to seal it up? I checked the back of the garage, and out bikes were still there. There was only one way to find out. I lifted the window about an inch and called out, "Chris?"

"Yeah, Jason. Get in here," Chris laughed. He sounded relieved.

He was relieved? Ha! It was nothing compared to how I felt. The lantern was burning and the place was quite cozy.

"That cop didn't catch you either I take it," said Chris smiling.

"No," I answered. I thought he was chasing you."

"Nope! Apparently he didn't chase either one of us. He sure scared the devil out of me though."

"Yeah, me too," I answered. "I was sure he caught you. What have you been doing all day?"

"Went back to the beach for a while looking for you, but didn't want to meet up with him again so I headed back here. Stopped on the way for a few munchies and then came back here to wait for you. Had no clue what I would do if you didn't show up."

"Have you checked your cell for messages?"

"No way! I don't want to hear the messages on my phone any more than you want to hear yours."

What a complete jerk I had been. How could I have doubted Chris? Not only had he come back to our hideout, but he brought goodies. He had bologna, crackers, cheese, and a gallon of milk. It was party time.

After we ate we just sat there and talked. "I wonder if we're pushing our luck hanging around this close?" I asked while wrapping myself up in one of the blankets.

"I was thinking about that today too. Maybe we should bike up the beach tomorrow and get a little further away.

"Sounds good to me, "I answered. "That cop spooked me today."

Chapter Four

That night we slept much better than the one before. We curled up in those blankets and actually kept pretty warm. When morning came we unlocked our bikes, tied a couple of the blankets on each of our straddle bars, hooked the lantern through my handle bars, and headed up the highway looking like the beach bums that we were. About noon we cut over at Madeira Beach to Alternate 19 and headed north to Clearwater.

By five o'clock we found ourselves at the pier watching the charter boats come in for the night. The weird stuff the fishermen come off the boat with has always intrigued me. We hung around for a couple of hours before deciding it was time to find a place to hole up for the night.

"Let's ride over to the beach to see if we can find a place to hide the bikes. Then I suppose we've got to find a place for us to stay," I mentioned to Chris as we left the pier.

Stowing the bikes turned out to be easier than we expected. Across the street was a little city park with a bike rack. We chained our bikes to the rack and headed down to the beach. As long as no one cut the chains or stole the wheels, we were golden.

We walked a mile or so up the beach and came across a group

of guys in their early twenties having a party. We strolled by minding our own business and tried to keep from getting clobbered by a flying Frisbee. Two of the younger ones of the group were lying on a blanket that we had to circle around to keep out of the line of fire.

The blond muscular one of the pair spoke as we passed, "Where are you two kids headed?"

"No where special," I answered. Just up the beach a ways.

"You hungry?" he asked. "You don't look like you've eaten for a while, and we do have some extra burgers."

"We haven't," Chris answered. "We've been riding all day and haven't stopped long enough to eat."

It wasn't just the riding all day that had stopped us, the fact that we were rapidly running out of money was the biggest reason.

We sat there for quite a while pigging out on their burgers, chips, and pop. Every once in a while a Frisbee would come our way and it was a mad scramble to see who would get it. The fact that we were ten years younger than most of them didn't seem to bother anyone. Everyone was friendly to us and seemed to be having a good time. We got a lot of smiles and our new friends got a bunch of funny grins that we didn't think a thing of until much later when we rehashed the night.

After it was too dark for Frisbee tossing, someone started a big bonfire. Three of the group had guitars with them and started harmonizing. The rest of us just sat around the fire and listened.

Around midnight I noticed that most of the group had scattered. If Chris and I were going to find a place to sleep off the beach, we had to get moving.

As we were getting ready to leave, Ron, the blond athletic looking one of the two that had actually invited us, leaned over and whispered, "Why don't you two wait for a couple more minutes. Almost everyone else has gone, and shortly it'll just be the four of us."

I didn't see anything wrong with that because he and his friend Sean had been awfully nice to us. The least we could do was hang around and keep them company a little longer. We didn't have anything better to do anyway, and we were kind of enjoying the fact that we didn't have any parents to answer to.

Within the next half hour the rest of the other small groups had gathered up their stuff and disappeared. As the last bunch left, one of them turned around and smirked, "You guys all have fun tonight."

I thought that was a rather strange comment, but then, I supposed that they were just being friendly thinking we were going to stay out half the night talking.

Leaning over on his elbow, Ron spoke rather softly, "Listen, you two. We have a little proposition for you. Since you're obviously run-a-ways with no place to go, why don't you come and spend the night with me and Sean. We have a motel rented just up the beach. It's not real fancy, but there are two beds and a shower. Jason, you can sleep with me, and Chris can sleep with Sean. If you cooperate there will be twenty dollars apiece for you in the morning. That will help tide you over for a couple of days and in the meantime, we can all have a great time tonight."

As he said that his hand slid up my leg above the knee. I jumped to my feet and blurted out, "Noooo! I think we had better go right now."

"Errr, Right! Chris stammered. Thanks for the food and everything tonight, but we've got to head out."

"Not so fast!" Ron growled as he grabbed me by the ankle and slammed me to the ground. Straddling me he put his left hand over my mouth and reached into his pocket. When his hand came out, there was a very large and sharp looking knife blade that popped out.

My eyes darted around in a panic. He was sitting on me and I couldn't move. I couldn't really see Chris it was so dark, but it looked like Sean was sitting on him too.

Ron snarled just loud enough for Chris and me to both hear, "Do you two know what a vet does when he neuters a male dog?"

We both nodded as we couldn't talk.

"I'm going to take my hand off your mouth now, and if there is one false move or even a squeak over a whisper by either of you, I'm going to pretend that you're both puppies. Understand?"

We both very helplessly nodded our understanding of the situation again.

"Ok, then, Puppy, come!" Sean snapped to Chris as he grabbed him by the wrist and half dragged him to this little overhang area that held back the high tide waters. Ron had be by the wrist too as we followed them dragging the blanket behind us. The area they took us was perfectly protected from the wind and prying eyes of anyone out for an evening stroll along the beach.

"Down, boy!" Ron commanded like I was some kind of dog. They both thought that was horribly funny. Chris and I were not laughing. Ron stuck his knife in the sand right beside the blanket where we could both see it. "You two sure are stupid. We could have gone back to our motel room where it is nice and comfortable and warm and all enjoyed ourselves while you earned yourselves some money. Too late now. You're going to suffer!"

The next half hour or so was horrible. They did things to us that I had never even heard of before. We were totally helpless because there wasn't a thing we could do to protect ourselves. We had made some bad choices that night and I never hurt so badly in my life.

They finally rolled us off their blankets and walked off laughing. We must have been in shock. Neither one of us spoke.

We just lay there in the sand for who knows how long. Suddenly I heard Chris crying. I crawled over to him and sat with him. Neither one of said a word. There was nothing we could do. We couldn't report them to the police even since we were run-a-ways ourselves.

Sometime later Chris quit sniffling and apparently dropped off to sleep. I did too somewhere along the line. In the morning we were at least talking and decided to go for a swim. Actually we weren't swimming. We just went out and sat in the salt water trying to sooth our aching bodies and cleanse ourselves the best we could. I never realized how much I could miss a shower.

The next few days were tough. Chris was depressed and didn't want to talk or eat. He wouldn't do anything except tear up at the most unexpected time. I began to worry about him big time. Instead of being full of great ideas about what to do next, he just followed me around with that hang dog expression on his face.

Friday night he started pacing. His mind was miles away and he avoided me. That was ok by me because it appeared like he was finally trying to work it out. Never the less, his strange actions kind of scared me.

Saturday morning came and he was a new person. Go figure! He laughed, cracked jokes, and picked on me for looking so tired.

"Listen," he told me. "I'm going up on the street and see what I can do about getting us something to eat. You wait right here and keep your eyes on our stuff, and I'll be right back. From the looks of you, you could probably use the time to catch a little more shuteye."

He stashed his backpack, emptied all his pockets, and handed me his money for safe keeping. He still had eight dollars and some change. I was confused, but not concerned. He had never done that before on any of his little excursions after free food, but I wasn't concerned. He acted pretty normal to me for the first time since...

As soon as he left, I cuddled up to my backpack behind our little sand bunker hide-away. Everything was going to be fine. I could relax finally.

I woke up with a start. A siren was headed this way with a steady weaper which meant something bad was going on. I panicked. Where the heck was Chris? I jumped up and headed for the street on a dead run. When I hit the parking area, I could see a crowd milling around out by the street. That siren was screaming in my brain.

I crashed through the crowd like a Sunday afternoon fullback. There was Chris lying against the curb covered with blood coming from a gigantic gash on his head. His right leg turned at a forty-five degree angle from his thigh. His left arm had a bone sticking right through the skin just above the elbow.

I dropped to my knees beside him and threw up. Some stranger pulled me to my feet and kind of held me. I buried my head in his chest and bawled. I knew Chris was dead.

By the time I pulled myself somewhat together, the ambulance attendants had scrapped him up and put him on a litter. I couldn't help but overhear some man in the crowd who saw it happen tell the same gruesome story to anyone who would listen.

"You wouldn't believe it," he proclaimed loudly. "I was standing right here waiting for the traffic to clear when this kid strolled up to the street and never slowed down. He never looked left or right, it was like he was in a daze, and he walked right in front of that pickup."

Yeah, I could believe it all right. He wasn't back to normal this morning after all. It was an act. He had decided during the night that he couldn't live with that humiliation any more. That's why he was so cheerful. He was going to escape.

When the paramedics were finally ready, I barged my way into the ambulance. I was going and they weren't going to stop me. Much to my surprise the attendant nodded towards a seat as if he expected me to go all along.

"Listen, his dad is a doctor at St. Petersburg Memorial Hospital. Take him there."

"That's a little further than the closest, but let's do it," the driver said. "Now, knock off the crying and talk to me. Your buddy is banged up bad, but he's alive."

"What's your friend's name, and what is his dad's name," he asked. When I told him, he called the hospital.

"St. Pete Memorial, Mercy Ambulance 4 in route with two adolescent males. One has been hit by a motor vehicle, and is in bad shape. The other is hysterical. Supposedly the injured one's name is Christopher Jackson, son of Dr. Jack Jackson—one of your attending physicians. We're probably ten minutes out."

I was holding on to my seat for dear life. That driver was traveling 80 with a steady weaper going. Traffic cleared out like you wouldn't believe, and I don't think we ever even slowed down. Someone must have notified the police en route to the hospital because there were traffic policemen at every light stopping the traffic and clearing the way for us.

We were only a couple of minutes out when a familiar voice came across the radio, "Mercy 4, what is the name of the hysterical adolescent?"

After the driver told him, Dr. Jackson said, "Jason, get a hold of yourself. When you get here I have a place reserved for you to wait outside of the normal waiting room. Mrs. Jackson is on her way and will sit with you. No more running away, you understand?"

I nodded and the driver told him I understood.

Chapter Five

They wheeled Chris through the swinging doors at the emergency room while I just stood there not having a clue. I was seriously thinking about ducking out and running, but I wasn't going to abandon Chris. Besides, I had promised Doc that I wouldn't.

Shortly some lady came up to me and asked, "Are you Jason?"

I told her yes and she led me to a small room inside of the emergency area and just left me. I paced the floor, I tried to sit. I couldn't. After an eternity, the door opened, and who should walk in but Mrs. Jackson. She walked across the room towards me. I just knew she was going to hit me right in the face. She wrapped her arms around me and hugged me. I did what any other red blooded American boy would do under the circumstances. I started bawling again. She just held me and let me get it out of my system.

We talked and time dragged on. I couldn't come out and tell her that he had done it on purpose or the reason why. It didn't matter. The only thing that mattered was that Chris was in good hands and hopefully would be okay. It seemed like an eternity again, but Doc finally walked in with a smile on his face.

"Chris is going to be okay. His body is broken up big time, but no major organs have been damaged and somehow he didn't hurt his head seriously other than that big cut and concussion. He's going to be in the hospital for a long, long time, but he's going to be okay."

I fell apart again and this time Doc held me. "Listen, we're all in the same boat. They won't let me in the operating room so I'll send aids out for cokes and we'll ride this out together."

"Jason, you have blood on your pants. Why?" Mrs. Jackson asked.

Doc turned me around and looked, and then said, "Okay, Jason, I want the entire story. Start at the beginning and don't leave anything out."

There was no way I could deny that man. The pain he was feeling was obvious. I told them everything from the moment we met Ron and Sean until now. My hands were visibly shaking I was so nervous telling them the story when Mrs. Jackson reached over and very gently placed her hands on mine. Tenderness and warmth were not something I was used to. It's funny too, because, believe it or not, I was more scared of Mrs. Jackson than I was Doc. If it hadn't been for me, none of this would have ever happened to Chris.

When I finished, Dr. Jackson said very matter of factly, "Before I call your dad, I'm checking you into the hospital for checking out the obvious, a complete physical, and observation for a couple of days. I think that while you are here I want a psychiatrist to take a look at you too.

"Why? I'm okay! I'm not going to do anything crazy or stupid. I'm telling you, Doc, I'm fine!"

"You probably are, but why take a chance on either your physical or mental well being? One never knows what kind of damage can come from an experience like you two had. Not only do you keep bleeding from the back end, you might also be bleeding mentally. Let's not take any chances."

"Okay, but do you have to call my dad? I'd rather just slip out the door and disappear than listen to what he's going to have to say. Do you realize how mad he must be at me for screwing up his plans?"

"That might be, but this whole thing has gone on long enough. Besides, I know your parents have been worried sick about you. Maybe now's the time that all of you can work out your differences and start accepting and enjoying each other like you should be doing. A part of somebody or the other's creed goes something like this, 'Help me accept those things I cannot change.' I think there is a message there for all of us. There is nothing I can say or do to change the fact that you and Chris ran away together and that he was badly injured, but I can accept that fact that you both had your reasons. I can also accept the fact that I had to be partially responsible for his decision, and I will do everything under my power to make sure he never has reason to make that choice again.

You have the same responsibility to your parents. You might not be able to change them, but you can accept the way they are and learn to live with them to the best of your ability."

"I guess the least I can do is try, Doc. I really will try."

Before I knew it I was in an examining room getting checked out and four stitches from where I was bleeding. As they were settling me in a room on the pediatrics floor, we heard someone over the PA announce, "Dr. Jackson, please report to the surgical lounge."

She didn't have to repeat it. Doc bolted out the door. Mrs. Jackson reached over and grabbed my hand and said, "come on. You're coming with us." Did you ever try running down a corridor with a hospital gown flopping open? How embarrassing!

It wasn't until we hit the elevator that Mrs. Jackson wrapped the darn thing around me and tied it shut.

When we arrived at the surgical lounge, the aide told us to go to Conference Room B that the surgeon would meet us there. I told them I would wait in the lounge knowing they would like to talk to him privately, but Mrs. Jackson grabbed my hand again and said, "We're all in this together, Jason. You come with us."

The accident pretty much mangled Chris. There were broken bones, bruises, scrapes, cuts, a concussion, you name it. He had it all. However, the doctor assured us that nothing was life threatening and he would be okay. He would be in recovery for at least two hours, and then they would send him to intensive care for who knows how long. After that he would have to spend weeks in the hospital recuperating. How long depended on how quickly he healed. The fact that he was young was in his favor. If he had been a little older, he would have probably been killed outright.

While he was in recovery room no once could see him and once he reached intensive care, only immediate family members could go in for just a few minutes at a time. So much for any ideas I had of seeing him that day.

Mrs. Jackson decided to take me back to my room so the nurse could do whatever she needed to do to finish settling me into my routine for the next few days. The nurse told me to go take a hot shower and put on those "sexy" hospital pajamas when I got out. At least they didn't fly open in the back.

I don't remember when anything felt as good as that shower. Neither Chris nor I had taken a shower since we left home. The closest we had come to bathing was soaking in the ocean, and that tended to leave you a little on the sticky side because of the salt.

It wasn't too long before I was sitting on my bed in hospital pajamas looking out the window. It had slipped my mind that Dr. Jackson said he was going to call my mom and dad. I was staring out the window enjoying the peace and quiet when they walked in. Mom raced over to me with tears in her eyes and kissed me. I don't remember the last time she did that. Dad smiled and stuck out his hand.

My homecoming, so to speak—even if it were in my hospital room, was altogether different than what I had expected. There was no yelling, no hitting, no Mom going to bed to close the door and read so she could block everything out. Also, they hadn't left for Michigan and left me behind. My parents actually acted human.

Naturally, they wanted the whole story too. I didn't pull any punches. I started back with the original decision to leave and told them everything. It took almost three hours to tell it all. They sat right there and listened. The only interruption we had was when Dr. Jackson came in and explained his role in putting me in the hospital. He said that he would like to give me a complete physical and take care of me, but if there was a family doctor or pediatrician they would prefer, that would be okay too. Whoever they chose, though, he would like to have the option of consulting with him. He was taking a personal interest in my case.

Dad was the most agreeable that I've ever seen him. He said that since Dr. Jackson knew all the particulars, he would prefer for him to take care of me rather than bringing in someone else. Also, he was agreeable to which ever child psychiatrist Doc wanted to recommend. I suspicion that the fewer people who knew what had happened to me the better as far as he was concerned.

After I finished telling my story, Mom and Dad went down to the admitting office to show their insurance card and do everything the correct way. When they left, they said that they would be back after dinner to see me again.

It wasn't too long after they left that Dr. Jackson came in with his little black bag, closed the curtain around the bed, and said, "Let's get started, Jason. This is going to take a while."

I have never been examined before or since the way I was that afternoon. He thumped, poked, prodded, and looked at every square inch of my body from the top of my head to the bottom of my feet—including the darned stitches that were starting to itch. He missed nothing.

He smiled a lot and joked with me all the time he was checking me over, which helped because I was pretty nervous. He told me exactly what he was going to do and why before each and every procedure. He even told me a couple of times that something might be uncomfortable—and it was. At least there were no surprises that way.

I don't know how he did it, but when he stuck that little flashlight thingie in my right ear, he told me to turn my eyes to the left and look at the wall. He made some crack about how the light was shining through the hole in my head and hitting the wall. It was good for a laugh anyway. Made me a little more relaxed about everything he was doing.

Everything he did wasn't that much fun especially when he was checking over the stitched area. Even though he was extremely gentle and soft spoken, that hurt. Finally he was done.

"I think you're in fine physical shape. Of course I won't know the total picture until I see the results of your urinalysis and blood tests. From all appearances you came through your ordeal with flying colors. There are a couple of spots that are pretty painful right now, and those will feel better within the next few days. The good thing is there is nothing seriously wrong."

Everything he told me confirmed what I was actually

43

feeling—essentially everything was okay. It's always a relief to hear good news because doctors tend to make me nervous. As long as the blood tests came out okay, I was fine physically. The next step was the shrink. He was going to check in on me in the morning. If everything went well there, he would discharge me in the next couple of days.

He wanted to make sure I had a couple of days with complete rest along with the traditional three square meals a day. Wonder what ever gave him the impression that maybe our eating and sleeping habits might be slightly out of sync with the rest of the world lately?

Chapter Six

That night Mom and Dad came back to the hospital to visit and brought me a chocolate shake. Not that I'm a chocoholic or anything, I just love chocolate. I relished that shake. Dad wanted to talk about the move to Michigan. He promised me that as soon as we arrived, he would sign up at a mental health clinic to work on his drinking problem and his apparent inability to get along with me.

That was the first time I ever heard him admit that he had a problem. As far as our relationship went, he always blamed me. He also said something else that floored me. He had joined a child abuse clinic and spent an hour or two every night getting counseling, answering the phones, and doing other things around the center. He was trying to get his life and problems under control.

The next morning my psychiatrist, Dr. Ben Michaels, stopped in. He spent two hours with me while I told him everything that had happened. He seemed a lot more interested in my relationship with my father and his treatment of me than in what had happened at the beach. When I told him about our encounter with the guys at the beach, his first question was how my dad reacted when I told him. Then he wanted to know how I thought he would have reacted if it had happened a month earlier before we ran away.

It was hard for me to be totally honest with all my answers because I had the gut level feeling that somehow Dad blamed me for the incident, and for some reason or the other, I needed to protect him. I guess I probably soft pedaled some of my answers trying not to make him look like the complete jerk that he was.

Doc Michaels was pretty clever though because he kept coming back to the same questions over and over only stated differently each time. "How did you feel about...What did you think about...What was going through your mind...How angry are you now talking about this..." When I thought about our conversation later that night, I realized he tricked me into answering some of those questions differently depending on what mood he got me in. I also realized that I had a bunch of anger bubbling away that I never realized I had. Doc Michaels seemed to be pushing that too.

After Doc Michaels left, the rest of the day went pretty smoothly. Dr. Jackson came by twice to stick his head in the door to see how things were going. The ward nurse popped in with an ice cream cone that afternoon right after Doc Jackson left. "Don't tell the boss that I'm sneaking you in ice cream during the afternoon," she smirked as she looked over her shoulder. I know darned well that he suggested it or she wouldn't have done it, but we had fun with the conspiracy aspect of it.

The next day I was going to bug Dr. Jackson about getting me out of the hospital. I couldn't get out of there fast enough to suit me. Between the needles, the exams, the questions, the lack of modesty, and everything else, I wouldn't have any regrets about leaving. I was bored to death.

Doc was there bright and early in the morning so I started

pumping him, "What about Chris? Am I going to see him before I leave? What's going on? Nobody is telling me anything. Every time I ask about him the subject gets changed."

Doc gave a big deep sigh, "Chris hasn't wakened from the surgery. That's why he's been in intensive care and you haven't been able to see him. We think it's a light coma and that he just isn't ready to wake up yet. This morning they moved him to a regular room down the hall. I've been talking to a couple of other doctors and everyone agrees that maybe we should let you go talk to him. Maybe it'll help. Who knows? All I know is that he is just lying there unresponsive."

"Can we go now?" I completely forgot asking about leaving. This was more important.

"Why not? Let's go."

We stopped outside of his room and Doc said, "I'm going to go and take care of my rounds. You go ahead inside, sit down beside him and just talk to him just like he was awake. You can tell him anything that's on your mind, but keep in mind he may hear you and remember what you say even if he doesn't wake up for a while."

Suddenly I was scared. I didn't know what to say. I tip toed across the room and sat down on the chair beside his bed. He looked terrible. He was covered with casts, bandages, tubes, you name it. What little skin you could see here and there was discolored with bruises and skid marks. I thought I was going to throw up again. It didn't help that my mind flashed back to him lying on the curb all bloody and in a heap. I started to cry.

"This is all my fault. If you hadn't gone with me this never would have happened. I'll never forgive myself. I know that when you wake up you're going to hate me." I went on and on in the same vein for who knows how long. I had my head down on the side of his bed and sobbed into his sheets as I poured out my heart.

"Will you shut up and quit blubbering," Chris mumbled out of the blue.

I snorted blowing snot, spit and tears all over his bed and started laughing. Underneath all that hospital crap was the same old Chris. He moved his hand out from under the covers and I grabbed it. He was awake. I was laughing and crying all at the same time.

After I finally got myself together a little, and Chris's voice was getting a little stronger, he said, "Pretty stupid wasn't I, Jason?"

"Nobody ever claimed that you were the brightest bulb in the socket," I laughed trying not to let him go and get too serious on me. He could save that for Dr. Michaels. The longer we talked the more wake and stronger he seemed. I didn't want him to go back to sleep until Dr. Jackson came in and saw him.

"So, Chris, how are you actually feeling under all that crap. Hopefully not as bad as you look." I couldn't help picking on him just a little.

"Not all that bad considering. They've got me all doped up so I don't feel any pain—but I'm really tired and it's hard to keep my eyes open. This whole thing has been kind of surreal. I've been awake and knew when Mom and Dad were here as well as all the doctors and nurses, but I was so dopy and tired, I just couldn't wake up. It was like a blanket of fog or something over me. Dad was always sneaking in and asking, 'How you doing little buddy? When you going to wake up and talk to me?' but I couldn't. I could hear him and just couldn't wake up. I was just too tired. Mom's a mess every time she comes in, and I've been half ticked because you never came around."

"They wouldn't let me. I kept asking about you and nobody ever told me what was going on until just before I came in today and your dad told me that you were in a light coma and wouldn't wake up. The quacks all got together and decided to let me come in to see if my being here would wake your dumb butt up."

"So where've you been all this time?"

"I was in a room too down the hall. If I'd known you were so close I would have sneaked in. However, I guess you weren't here until this morning"

"Why, how come they have you here? I'm the one that got clobbered by a truck."

"Now don't get jealous just 'cause I've had a little special attention too. I rode the ambulance here with you, and your dad checked me in for a few days for observation after our little episode with those two clowns down on the beach. Then, of course, that stupid stunt you pulled earned me a visit with one of the local head doctors. Actually, I think he was trying to keep me out of my old man's hands for a few days."

"Who's your regular doctor? Is it Dad?"

"Yes, and he's been great. He gave me the most complete physical you ever saw and has been treating me mostly for bruises and checking to make sure I don't get any kind of disease from those guys."

"Dad's known for being thorough according to Mom. I don't know what all they've done to me. I don't remember all the details 'cause things have been so foggy. So what else has happened?"

Well, last night your dad chewed me out for not wearing those gorgeous hospital pajamas. He caught me standing in front of the window looking out in nothing but my skivvies. I don't think he liked that too well. I don't know why not. I wasn't flashing the people in the parking lot or anything.

Chris Laughed. "He's always been like that. Just because he turn's the furnace off at night, he figures everyone will catch pneumonia if they're not all bundled up. I guess that's one of the disadvantages of having M.D. tacked on to your dad's last name.

I don't know how long we talked, but we were both laughing at something silly when Mr. and Mrs. Jackson both raced in. Chris and I had been having so much fun I forgot to tell anyone that he was awake. He was definitely going to need clean sheets because after I had slobbered all over them, Mrs. Jackson did it again.

It wasn't long before they kicked me out saying Chris had to get some rest. I think that was just an excuse to get rid of me. He'd been sleeping for almost a week. Later in the afternoon I sneaked out of my room and went down to his. He was sleeping. Rats!

Later I asked the head nurse if I had to get permission to go down there. She said it would be ok as long as the door was open. She said that if he was asleep, the curtain was drawn, or the door was closed to just leave and come back later. That was fine with me. After dinner I went down again and his mom and dad were there so I just said, "Hi!" and left. Before they left they came down to see me for a little while. That was neat. They had both visited me daily before Chris woke up, but I figured they'd spend all their spare time with him now.

"Hi, sweetie," Mrs. Jackson said as she kissed me on the head. Mr. Jackson came over to the bed and gave me a hug. I teared up again. I just wasn't used to parental types acting like they actually cared for me.

Doc hugged me again and laughed, "Oh boy! Just what we need—two going through puberty at the same time. By the way, you think you might be ready to leave this place tomorrow afternoon?"

With that to look for, I was all smiles after that. They stayed for a little while longer—visiting hours were actually over by then, but it was ok. When they left I thought that maybe I would be able to sleep. I don't know when I had my last really good night's sleep. I was always waking up on and off all night long.

The next morning after breakfast I went down to see Chris. He was watching TV. "Turn that stupid thing off," he said. "We've got a lot to catch up on."

I sat down beside him in the chair and couldn't help getting serious. "Do you realize how lucky you are to have the parents you do? They both have been around to see me more often than my own. They even care. One day I was a little depressed when your dad came in during his rounds. He sat down and talked to me for a good half hour. He started picking on me giving me a hard time. He was just trying to get me out of my funk. It worked. He even gave me a hug before he left. You know, he's so soft spoken and sincere. I suppose there are times when he yells and screams and maybe even swats your butt, but I'll bet it's a rare exception to the rule."

"Jason, the only complaint I have ever had about my dad is the fact that I don't see enough of him. Four or five days go by when I don't even see him. He's always at this darn hospital. He gets up and leaves before I'm up in the morning and doesn't get home until after I've gone to bed."

"I bet that will change. It really bothered him to think that you'd walk out in front of a truck before you talked things over with him. He kind of let that slip out one night about eleven when he came in and was giving me a hard time about not sleeping. I asked him what the heck he was doing there so late and that's when he sat down and talked for a while."

About that time the head nurse burst into the room, "thought I'd find you down here. You've got an appointment with Doctor Michaels and then your parents are coming in to take you home. Your luxury vacation tour of our facility is over. Tell Chris goodbye, and you come with me."

"See you later, Chris. I'll try to get back tomorrow."

"Ok, see you later."

When I reached the door, I kind of turned around and waved.

He smiled back under that white turban wrapped around his head and waved back. Did it ever seem good to be able to talk to him again even if it were here in a depressing hospital room.

Dr. Michaels was in my room when the nurse and I got back. He stayed and we talked for over an hour. Before he left, he told me," I know your dad is putting forth an effort to change his own feelings and behavior towards you, but don't expect too much too soon. But I'm telling you right here and now, you haven't had your last beating. He will slip and blow a fuse and you are his target. The main thing is that you have to do your part to try to keep him defused. Hopefully over time it will get better."

"I think it's going to be okay. He's already changed one-hundred percent. Sure, there will be some rough spots, but he's talking to me now for the first time. He even smiled at me once."

"It's a step in the right direction, but don't get your hopes up too high. I certainly hope you are right, but these things take time. People do not make permanent changes in their self control overnight. I want to see you once a week for a few weeks just to monitor how things are going. I'll set that up with your parents. In the meantime, Jason, good luck and we'll see you next week."

After the shrink left I dressed into my own clothes. Mom had taken all my grubby stuff out in a trash bag and brought me clean to go home in.

Chapter Seven

My parents checked me out of the hospital, and we headed for home. "Since we are so close to the beach, do you suppose we could check to see if our bikes are still where we left them?" I asked my dad.

"I don't see why not. I'll bet they aren't there though."

"I'm hoping. We had them chained up together pretty good to a metal post."

What a surprise! There they both were untouched. While Dad was getting them into the trunk, I slipped down the beach to where we had stowed our back packs. That was a bit too much to ask, but I'd never have known for sure if I hadn't checked. They were gone. Probably the beach cleanup crews had picked them up and thrown them away.

Chris was happy to get his bike back too even if he wouldn't be able to ride it for a while. He would probably stay in the hospital four to six weeks and keep that bad leg in a cast for up to three months provided everything went well.

That sucked big time for him. I wasn't happy about it either. By the time he got out and was ready to actually be out and about I'd be gone. Dad rescheduled our move for the week after Christmas. That would be vacation time at school. Bummer!

Going back to school was going to be strange. I had been out for a couple of weeks and had missed a lot of work. There would be tons of questions from friends about the two of us—some of which I would never answer. Dad scheduled a meeting for Friday afternoon at 2:30 before I was due back on Monday. I'm sure the teachers were all thrilled to death over that one. They usually raced us out the door on Friday afternoon—not really, but close to it.

Dad segued into his lawyer mode and took over the meeting as soon as he was introduced by the principal. Kind of interesting. I had no idea what was to come—he hadn't said a thing. "Gentlemen and ladies, I will be brief and to the point. Jason has been out of school for a couple of weeks now due to his own volition and poor judgment. His mother and I are requesting that you provide him with each and every assignment that he has missed. For all intents and purposes, he is grounded until he catches up each and every one of them. While this is going on I expect him to keep up with his daily work. What you do with those back assignments is up to your own discretion. Whatever you decide will be fine with me; partial credit, no credit, full credit, whatever. The only thing I ask is that you keep track and email me with a progress report weekly until all is caught up. Are there any questions?"

Grounded? What a rip! That wasn't fair. He could have at least given me advanced warning. I must have had a funny look on my face because he turned to me and said, "What about you? Do you have anything to say?"

"No, sir," was all I could squeak out. He was punishing me in public which I just hated. I was totally embarrassed.

I think the teachers all noticed my discomfort because nobody really looked right at me or said a thing. A couple of them kind of patted me on the shoulder as they filed out, but it was pretty quiet.

That weekend I was allowed to go see Chris everyday for a couple of hours, but I wasn't allowed out of sight other than that. I was grounded! Probably forever.

Monday morning finally arrived and I rode my bike to school like always. I locked it up at the bike rack and noticed several kids watching and probably talking about me. It was uncomfortable, but there was nothing I could do except try to act normal.

I walked into my first hour English class and Mr. Rogers had all my assignments waiting for me.

"Hi, Jason. Good to have you back," he smiled at me as he said it like he actually meant it.

"Thanks, Mr. Rogers. It's been a long time hasn't it? Looks like I've missed six months of work instead of a couple of weeks."

"Well, the world didn't come to a screeching halt waiting for you, I can tell you that. Now, when you get to some of these grammar assignments—especially the participle phrases—feel free to come in early or after school so I can help you with them. I also wrote down my Email address so you can get a hold of me that way too."

"Thanks," I said. "I've always done ok in English, but I'm sure I'll need some help getting all this."

All the teachers were very nice that day. They all had my assignments ready and offered their help. I was going to be a busy, busy boy for awhile.

Some of our friends were the same as always. Lots of them had a lot of questions about how Chris was doing. The doctors hadn't let him have any outside visitors – namely kids – so no one had talked to him. Some of the kids were kind of strange acting though. Those kids seemed to actually avoid me like I had the plague or something. One kid even made a crack about Chris's accident being my fault. If he hadn't been helping me out of a jam, he never would have gotten hurt.

I tried to ignore their comments, but they bothered me. I didn't want to react to something like that right away. I'd had enough problems dealing with that in my own mind. Chris didn't blame me, but I did, and if the kids dissed me too much on that one, someone might get punched.

Tuesday night Dr. Jackson had to go the hospital for a short while so he took me along and dropped me off at Chris's room while he did his thing. After I told Chris about Friday's meeting with the teachers, I broached the subject again. "Chris, we haven't talked about this since you came out of your coma, but now that it's been a while, how responsible do you think I am for your accident now?"

"What do you mean?" he questioned. "I don't think I understand what you are talking about."

"If I hadn't talked you into going with me, none of this would have happened. Some of the kids at school seem to think it's all my fault. I hadn't even considered the fact that other people might blame me for what happened until they started mouthing off about it. After we talked before, I've just thought all along that it just happened, and it wasn't really either one of our faults. Was I wrong?"

"That's a bunch of bull crap and you know it! If you remember right, it was my idea to go to the beach. If there is anyone to blame, it's those Ron and Sean characters, and not you. You just tell those so called classmates of ours at school for me that they can just cut out that kind of talk. Dr. Michaels said that neither one of us have to be saddled with any feelings of guilt or blame."

"We really haven't talked about our Shrink. How do you like Dr. Michaels anyway?"

"He's kind of neat for a psychiatrist, except he has some really weird ideas. He mentioned you a couple of times and then told me, 'What a nice boy you are.' When I stuck my finger down my throat and gagged he thought I was serious so I had to straighten him out and told him that you and I were best friends and practically like twins."

"Yeah, I told him the same thing. He seems to think our relationship is very important and he worries about it. I've told him a couple of times that we're fine."

Mom was pretty decent while Chris was in the hospital. She let me go to the hospital after school. I did my homework there and explained the assignments to him. Actually we worked together. I helped him with his math and science, and he helped with the English and social studies. Worked well for both of us. The visiting teacher came three times a week and timed it so I would be there at the same time. We both polished off those missing assignments pretty quickly.

Several times in the evening Dr. Jackson picked me up when he had to run over to the hospital for a while. I'm not sure, but I think he was just getting me out of my detention. A couple of times he just went up and visited Chris with me. He really had no reason to go to the hospital. Doc and I got to know each other really well during this time. Both of us kind of talked non-stop. I was more comfortable around the Jacksons than I was at home.

Dad pretty much ignored me. He wasn't mean or anything, he just didn't seem to want anything to do with me. One night after dinner Dad sat down and buried his face in the newspaper like he did every night he was home. All of my back homework assignments were finished so I was working on an extra credit project for social studies.

I was tired of the silent treatment so I looked up from my project, "Dad, when I was in the hospital, Mom said you were going to a child abuse center nights to answer phones, join in with the discussion groups, and help out around there. Since I've been home, you haven't gone once. Any reason?"

He set the paper down and glared at me just like he used to do, "Why? Do you think I need it? I haven't laid a hand on you since you've been home. Why'd you ask?"

"No particular reason. I just thought of it, and knew you hadn't been going. I was just curious, I guess."

"If you must know, I don't have a problem like some of those weirdoes down there. Just because I've always beaten your butt for you when you deserved it, doesn't mean I abused you."

That's not what Dr. Michaels said. He said Dad was sick and that he might never be cured.

I don't know what ever possessed me to open my mouth, but I couldn't resist, "What about all those times when I didn't deserve it? What about all those time when you were just drunk and ugly and wanted to beat up on someone, and I was elected?"

He never tolerated my smart mount and this was no exception. He bolted out of that chair and was across the room in two steps and blasted me with an open handed right hook across the face. I crashed in a heap on the floor and he was on top of me before I bounced twice.

He screamed at me, "Worthless mouthy, queer bait brat...screwed up my career...should have moved months ago...all your fault!"

All the time he screamed these insanities at me, he hit me again, again, and again. Most of the blows landed on my face or head, but some of them were on various other parts of the body. I tried to cover up and roll out of there, but I couldn't budge his weight. I just covered up and protected myself the best I could. Finally he stopped.

"Go to bed, you useless piece of crap!" he gasped all out of breath. "Get out of my sight!"

He didn't have to tell me twice. I left all my stuff right where it was and headed for my room. I didn't even take time to wash my face which was bleeding quite steadily from the nose. I just stripped down to my boxers and crawled into bed with toilet paper stuffed into my nose.

Later—maybe ten minutes later—Dad walked into my room. He was very, very quiet and calm, and that in itself scared me. That was not normal.

He clicked on my light and walked over to the chair and sat down. It was then that he spoke, "Son, get out of bed and come over here. I want to talk to you."

That was eerie. I didn't know what he was up to, but I did as I was told without a word. I didn't want to set him off again. He didn't even seem to notice the bloody TP sticking out of my nose.

"You disobeyed me again," he said very softly. "You have been told time after time not to leave things out when you finish with something. The kitchen table is a mess."

He forgot that he had run me off himself. He was so calm and collected when he spoke, I had no idea what was going on until he continued. "You are going to have to clean up your mess in the kitchen before you go back to bed. However, before you do, you are going to be punished. You have to learn to follow the rules, and that is all there is to it."

With that he took me by the arm and turned me over his knee and spanked me like I was about five years old. Dad was nuts. If he didn't get help soon, he was going to kill me.

I went out to the kitchen and cleaned up my mess. Then I went back to bed wondering what I was going to do. I had to get out of that house. I was tired of hurting. I didn't dare look in the mirror.

Shortly afterwards Mom came home from where ever she had been. They talked quietly for a while and then the two of them left. They probably thought I was sleep because they didn't even tell me they were leaving.

As soon as they were out the door, I dressed and headed out. If they were out drinking, I sure wasn't going to hang around for another beating when he came home drunk. I had to talk to someone so I headed for the Jackson's. Hopefully at least one of the Jacksons was home. Both had told me if I ever need to vent or just talk to come over anytime of the day or night. Maybe they would have some ideas because I wasn't going back home.

Mrs. Jackson opened the door, gasped out loud, and grabbed me and pulled me into her. "Jack! Come here quick!" she yelled out to Doc. "What happened? Was it your dad?"

She was holding me and I was bawling and blowing snot, blood, and tears all over her. I hadn't realized what a mess my face was. They took me into the kitchen and sat me down. The floor had linoleum so at least I wouldn't bleed all over the carpet.

"Go get the camera, would you please?" he asked Mrs. Jackson. I didn't get it at first, but what he wanted was proof of extreme abuse. She came back with the camera and started snapping pictures. They took off my shirt which was covered in blood anyway and took several more. Before they started cleaning me up, Doc excused himself and went to make a phone call.

When he came back he started cleaning me up while I told them the whole story. They couldn't believe it. "You are not going back there tonight or maybe forever. I've called a Mrs. Stevens who I know from Child Protective Services and she's on her way over to get you. She'll take you someplace that is safe until they decide what to do."

"could I just stay here?" I asked.

"I wish you could, but if your dad came looking for you, I would have to turn you over to them legally. This way he won't be able to find you and you'll be protected," he explained.

I wasn't crazy about the idea of going to some strange place, but I couldn't go back home now if I wanted to. Dad would come home drunk, out of control, and I would just have to go through the whole thing again. No thanks!

While we were waiting for Mrs. Stevens, Mrs. Jackson took me into the bathroom and told me to jump in the shower. While I was letting the water beat on me she came back in with clean clothes that belonged to Chris and picked up all my stuff and disappeared. That was the first really good look I had of myself. Both eyes were black and blue, by face was all scratched and bruised, and my nose was a mess. My whole upper body was bruised, scraped, and sore. I was one handsome dude that night.

When I got out of the shower Doc smeared antiseptic all over my face and upper body. Stuck on a couple of bandages here and there, and checked my nose. That's when he decided it was broken. Gave me a couple of children's Tylenol, and then we waited for Mrs. Stevens.

Mrs. Stevens was very nice but all business. Doc showed her the digital images of the pictures so she could verify that they hadn't been doctored. She wanted him to take some more of me now that I had showered for comparison. My black eyes were starting to swell shut and she wanted that. She also asked him to take pictures of my bloody clothes. While she was talking to me, he took the camera to his den and printed all the pictures and gave them to her. My life was about to take a big turn. Who knew if it would be for the better or worse.

Chapter Eight

Mrs. Stevens took me to a professional foster care center for kids in trouble. It was only three blocks from the hospital where Chris was. She ordered me not to go to school until further notice and that a home bound teacher would come. She told me to pretty much stay out of sight. However, I could go to the hospital to see Chris during the day.

There were several rooms upstairs with single beds and chests for clothes. They told me that I was more or less expected to stay in my room except for meals. There were all kinds of magazines and books and an old analog TV for me to amuse myself with. I hate TV and the magazines and books were all old. I was the only kid there at the time so I had no one to talk to except for Mrs. Boardman the lady who ran the place.

She told me that Mrs. Stevens and others had dropped off literally hundreds of kids over the years. "The usual stay here is three days. Juvenile Court will decide what is going to happen to you. You will either go back home or you will go to a permanent foster home or you will go to the juvenile home."

"I'm not going home!"

"You won't have any say in it. The majority of you kids go to the Juvie home for at least a while and then get farmed out from there."

I think she thought I was some kind of gangster. I sure hoped the courts wouldn't think so too.

Sleep didn't come too easily that night. In fact, I tossed and turned most all night. I couldn't have much more than dozed off when Mrs. Boardman called me for breakfast. Two bowls of oatmeal and three slices of toast later, I felt semi-human again. The rest of the day was pretty boring because I spent most of it in my room. Mrs. Stevens didn't want me leaving the house just in case someone wanted to get a hold of me. Besides, as Mrs. Boardman put it, "Normal kids are in school and not out roaming the streets looking for trouble."

A day or so later Dr. Jackson stopped by to see if I wanted to go see Chris. "Doc, my face looks so bad I don't want Chris to see me like this."

"Why? He knows all about it and has been hassling his mom and me about getting you up there. He's very upset about what has happened and wants to see you. Besides you don't look as bad as you did a couple of days ago."

Mrs. Stevens hadn't told the Boardmans about Doc and Mrs. J so she was suspicious of him. She called protective Services to see if it were okay for him to take me out of the house. I suppose it was the proper thing to do, but it seemed pretty lame that she wouldn't trust a licensed MD driving a brand new Lexus.

Doc wasn't bothered about it at all, "Jason, if she hadn't checked me out I would have reported her to Protective Services. Suppose I had really been your dad trying to smuggle you out of here."

"I wouldn't have gone!"

"That's what you say, but if he threatened you, what then?"

"I don't know."

"That's what I thought. By the way, you and Mrs. Stevens hadn't been gone thirty minutes when your dad showed up. He was in tears and all shook up over what had happened. He had hurt you and you had run away again and he didn't know what he was going to do.

"I told him right off that you hadn't run away. You came to our house looking for help, and I called Protective Services, and they took you into their custody.

"He didn't seem upset by that in the least. He said he needed help. He said you frustrated him so, he just went nuts. Then he shook his head and said you'd be safer someplace else for a while. He said he loves you, but couldn't stop himself from beating you up."

"What a cop out! He doesn't love me. He never has. He doesn't want me around. He'd love it if the state would take me off his hands."

"I don't think so. I think he's a very emotionally shook up and frustrated man right now."

"Yeah, at my expense."

"I hate to see you so bitter about your dad, but I do understand. It's just that you're so full of hate and that's a terrible feeling to have. I know Chris gets mad at me sometimes, and it scares me to think that he could ever feel the way you do."

"You sure don't have to worry about Chris feeling like me. His only complaint is that you're working at the hospital all the time and he never sees you. That's why he ran away with me hoping that if you missed him, you'd understand how he feels."

"Is that the straight scoop? Part of the reason he ran away is because I'm working 12-14 hours a day?"

"That's right, but I wasn't supposed to be the one to tell you. He's been waiting for just the right time to say something. He's afraid that you'll get all mad at him."

"No way! I wish I'd known long ago. I do appreciate your telling me though, and I won't let on that you ever said a word if that makes you feel any better."

"I really appreciate that. Can we talk about something else for a minute before we get there?"

"Sure, what's on your mind?" Doc asked.

"Doc, what are they going to do with me? I'm scared! Mrs. Boardman says they only keep kids there at her place for two or three days max and then they're shipped out. She said I'd probably end up in the juvie home for a while. I don't want to go there, but I'm not going home either. I'm so confused, I guess I don't know what I want. However, where I end up isn't what bothers me the most."

"What is bothering you? You've acted like you had something else on your mind since I picked you up."

"I'm afraid that I'm going to lose you, Mrs. Jackson, and Chris. You are the only people that really mean anything to me in the whole wide world, and now I'm going to lose you."

"You aren't going to lose us. We'll keep in touch no matter what. I know the judge has a lot of experience in these types of things and he's going to do what is best for you. And, you can rest assured; the juvenile home is not what is best for you. In the meantime, quit worrying. If you don't you'll have an ulcer before you ever reach thirteen," he grinned as he said it. "Things will work out for the best."

When doc looked at his watch he said that we'd been in the parking lot for over an hour talking, and, "I suppose we should probably go up and see Chris, hadn't we?"

"I guess, but can we kind of keep my problems away from him for now? He's got enough to worry about just getting himself better."

"Hey! He already knows everything. We haven't kept any

65

secrets from him. It's just been driving him nuts that we haven't got you up here yet."

When we got to Chris's room, Doc let me go in by myself for awhile first while he checked charts on the computer. I just don't think he wanted to be there when Chris gave me the third degree about my face. I'd forgotten that my face was such a mess when I asked him not to mention it to Chris.

I hadn't even got all the way in the room when Chris blurted out, "That's garbage! Your old man's totally evil. I knew you were going to look bad, but this is terrible! You look like the devil!"

"Thanks! That makes me feel a lot better."

"He's nuts. You've got to get out of that house permanently before he kills you. Sit down and tell me everything."

Not too much later Doctor Jackson wandered in. "Dad, can't you do anything constructive for Jason? Why can't he come live with us? Nobody's going to be using my bed for awhile. As far as that goes, he could sleep in the guest room or someplace. He was safer in his sleeping bag under my bed than he is at home, and you just can't let him go to the juvie home."

"Chris, all these things take time. Jason is safe right now, and that's the important thing. I'm sure the courts will force his dad to get help before he ever goes back home."

The next couple of weeks proved interesting as well as slow. I went back to school. Mrs. Boardman drove me back and forth. I had some freedom then because I could go out and didn't have to stay in my room all the time. Somehow, I managed to carry a B average at school through all the turmoil. I wouldn't swear to it, but I think I received a few early Christmas presents from my teachers.

Life smoothed out for me. Chris had a hospital bound teacher who he thought was a little on the stupid side. So every day when

Mrs. Boardman picked me up at school, she would drop me off at the hospital for a couple of hours. I would help him with his assignments since we had all the same classes. Helping him helped me learn the stuff better too.

Chris's dinner always came right at five o'clock so that was a good time for me to head back to the Boardman's. It was only about a mile and a half so it was easy to walk. Several times, however, Doc Jackson just happened to be cruising in the area of Chris's room at five o'clock and ended up giving me a ride. Twice he and Mrs. Jackson dropped in about 4:30 to see Chris and took me out to eat when his dinner arrived. That was fine with Mrs. Boardman as long as Doc called to let her know. I guess she didn't trust my word. One Friday night they took me to a movie after dinner. They seemed to enjoy my company, and I definitely enjoyed theirs. It was kind of like a home life that I never had and always dreamed about.

The last time I saw Chris at the hospital was on Thursday, December 15th. The next day they sprang him for good. I wasn't going to be able to see him very much after that because the Boardman's lived too far from the Jacksons for me to walk, and I sure couldn't expect them to take me out of their way like that. They were getting paid to drive me back and forth to school, not take me out-of-the way to Jackson's and then sit in the driveway for an hour or so while I visited Chris. Besides, Winter Break from school was almost upon us, so they wouldn't be making that drive at all. I only had one more week of school before break. Wonderful! I expected to spend the whole break just sitting around in my room at the Boardman's.

Everything was up in the air anyway because a court date had finally been set for Monday the nineteenth. Some kind of determination was to be made about what was going to happen to me. On Friday I warned all my teachers that I probably wouldn't be back after vacation. However, I wanted to let them know that I wasn't running away again. I had learned my lesson on that score. None of them seemed real concerned. They all smiled and wished me luck. Mr. Rogers made a special point to tell me to keep my chin up between then and Monday. He said he was a great believer in the Spirit of Santa Claus, and he was sure everything would work out. It was almost as if he knew something.

Anyway, I certainly hoped he was right. My life had been goofed up enough the past few months without adding more problems. At that point I didn't much care what happened as long as it was relatively permanent, and I didn't have to go back home.

When the Boardman's got me to court on Monday, it looked like old home week. My parents, Dr. Jackson, my psychiatrist – Dr. Michaels, Mrs. Stevens, and a whole flock of other people that I didn't even know were all there sitting around a huge table. Apparently, it was not to be a trial like I had expected, but some kind of a meeting.

Somebody showed me where to sit when I arrive. The logistics of the seating arrangement were interesting to me. They had me on opposite ends of the table from my parents. Dr. and Mrs. Jackson sat on one side of me, and the judge sat on the other.

It appeared that all the arrangements regarding my future had all ready been made before I even got there. The judge looked over at me and started speaking, "Jason, a lot has happened in the short time you've been at the Boardman's. What I am about to tell you has been formally agreed upon and signed by everyone concerned. The purpose for you to be here today is to hear what decisions have been made regarding your future from me as your legal guardian in this matter.

"Your parents are leaving immediately after these proceedings for Michigan without you. You are as of this moment a ward of this court. You have been placed in a foster home immediately and indefinitely. I say indefinitely because your parents do have the option of reclaiming you at a later date, if and when certain conditions are met.

"Your dad realizes he has a problem that he cannot handle. It appears that his problem is only with you as he is not as he is not dangerous to society as a whole. Therefore, before he can reclaim you, he must attain a letter of certification from a qualified psychologist or psychiatrist stating that he has received proper treatment and is considered cured.

"That leaves us with the problem of what to do with you in the mean time. Doctor and Mrs. Jackson, with whom you are acquainted, have asked the court for custody of you until your father presents the court with the appropriate papers."

I could hardly believe my own ears. Dr. and Mrs. Jackson had asked for custody of me. They were going to be my new parents. I could barely contain myself. I wanted to jump up and down and yell, but I didn't dare.

The judge continued, "You are under complete control of the Jackson's and this court until further notice. I want you to understand that they have complete responsibility for your care, welfare, and well being. You will obey them as if they were your own parents. When you are punished, or you think you're getting a raw deal, you do not have the option to run away, mouth off, argue, or anything else. Is that understood?"

"Yes, Sir! I promise, I won't give them one speck of trouble."

"If for any reason or at any time you violate the trust I am putting you, you will be sent to the St. Petersburg Juvenile Detention Center until either your parents reclaim you, or you reach your nineteenth birthday. Is that understood?"

"Yes, Sir!" I answered again even more soberly than the last.

"Jason, do you have any questions of the court, your parents, or Doctor and Mrs. Jackson?"

"No, Sir," I answered softly.

The judge stopped and looked around at all of us sitting there. When no one else had any questions or comments either, he continued, "Therefore, this administrative hearing is adjourned."

With that he stood and walked out of the room. Everyone else stood quickly until he was gone. Then I walked over to Mom and Dad and said goodbye. Mom was in tears, and Dad was chewing his lip.

"Son," he said, "I'm so sorry it turned out this way. However, right now this is for the best. I don't hate you. I don't know why this has happened. I promise you, I will get help this time. Believe me."

I choked up and couldn't say anything, so I just shook hands with him, kissed Mom, and watched as they turned around and walked out the door. The tears streamed down my face. I was a complete failure as a son.

I felt a couple of arms drape over my shoulders. Doctor and Mrs. Jackson both had a hold of me and were smiling at me, "Let's go home," Doc said. "Chris is waiting for you."

On the way home they told me how all the details had been worked out. It seems the morning after the big blow up, Dad and Dr. Jackson went to Probate Court together to ask the judge to turn my custody over to the Jacksons. After that, it was just a matter of taking care of all the paper work and legal stuff. Nobody had told me for two reasons. If things didn't work out for some reason, they didn't want me to be disappointed. Secondly, the Jacksons wanted it to be a big surprise. Surprised, speechless, and thrilled – I pretty much didn't stop crying until we got home.

Chapter Nine

Chris met us at the door with his brand new walking cast. We greeted each other rather sloppily, and then Mrs. J grabbed me by the arm and hauled me into the bathroom and washed my face for me. I was a mess. Puberty sucks!

The four of us sat around the living room all talking non-stop until Mrs. Jackson finally decided to get some dinner going. That was good news because I was starved. The Boardmans had stopped at a hamburger joint for lunch on the way to the hearing but I had been too nervous to eat.

While she was starting dinner, Dr. Jackson suggested that Chris take me down the hall to show me our room. I couldn't believe my eyes. They had moved Chris's big double bed into the guest room and brought the two oversized twin beds in from there. My hang up stuff was on the right side of the walk in closet while Chris's stuff was on the left. There was also a dresser in there for all my other clothes.

"The right side of the desk is yours too," Chris told me as I was checking things out. Sure enough, my schools books and notebook were in the top drawer. The second drawer was full of paper, pencils, pens, and that sort of thing. The third drawer was empty.

"That's your junk drawer," Chris explained. "Now, before you do anything else, look under your bed."

Lying there was my sleeping bag that I had stashed under Chris's bed a couple of months earlier.

"Actually, you have to blame Dad's weird sense of humor for that one. It's been rolled up in the back of the closet all this time, but he thought it only fitting that you find it there."

Chris thought it was kind of corny, but I thought it was a pretty good joke. We had quite a while before dinner would be ready so we sat on our beds and tried to catch up on what had happened the past couple of weeks since I saw him last. He told me that Doc suddenly came to the conclusion that his working 12-14 hours a day was a type of abuse to his family too. Therefore he hired two associates to help him with his clinic. The understanding was that he left his office every day at four p.m., and they were to take care of any patients that were left and do the hospital visitations. Except for an actual life or death emergency, Doc was not to be bothered at home. As it worked out, the two new associates saw most of the patients while Doc acted more as a consultant than anything else. Needless to say, Chris was thrilled about the new arrangement. Me too because that that way I would get to see more of him too. Wonder if our little conversation outside of the hospital that night in the parking lot had anything to do with it?

The most meaningful event of the week came Monday night at dinner after we had come home from court. Mrs. Jackson said it was ridiculous for me to call the Dr. and Mrs. Jackson. So from then on they became Mona and Doc. At that point, I wouldn't have felt comfortable calling them Mom and Dad like Chris did, but that was close and I felt good about it.

A new set of house rules were set down for Chris and me to live by. I think they were harder on him than me because most of the things I already did. We had to make our beds in the morning and put our dirty clothes in the hamper, not throw them on the floor or under the bed. Bummer! Also, Chris and I had to clear the table, rinse the dishes, and put them in the dishwasher. Big deal! Half the time Mona helped. We also had to keep the lawn mowed and the garden weeded as needed.

I don't think any week ever went as fast for me as that one did. With all his new found free time, Doc decided to make up for some of the things he had missed. He took us to a crab leg and shrimp buffet on Wednesday night. That was something I had never done with my parents. The high school basketball team was playing in a Christmas tournament that week so we went to all of their games. It seemed like we were on the go all week.

When we went to bed on Christmas Eve after church, the tree was pretty barren underneath. Christmas morning came and I planned on staying in bed until they had their Christmas. I didn't want to horn in on that. I didn't expect any gifts except for the couple of things my parents had shipped from Michigan. Chris tried to get me up, but I just rolled over and pretended to go back to sleep. After a few futile tries he left me alone. I did go back to sleep.

Suddenly Doc burst into the room, grabbed my foot, and literally dragged me out of bed and onto the floor. He looked down at me grinning. "Now, are you going to get your tail in gear and come out to see what Santa brought, or do I have to drag you all the way skidding your behind across the carpet?"

"I'll come peacefully," I laughed as I dressed in a hurry and headed for the living room.

The tree was beautiful and so was everything underneath. My parents had sent some clothes and things along with a letter wishing me a Merry Christmas. The Jacksons had hidden all the gifts they had bought for Chris and me until Christmas morning.

We had exactly the same number under the tree. I'd be willing to bet the dollar amount came within five dollars too. Doc and Mona were quite a pair. Christmas was fun.

School started again the Monday after New Years, but I had to go by myself. The doctors wanted Chris to wait one more week before he went back. He seemed to be getting along fine to me, but I suppose they knew best. That night Chris and I walked into the living room after finishing dishes. Doc looked up from his Sudoku puzzle book and asked, "What's for home work?"

Since Chris and I had the same classes, I was to bring the assignments home and explain them to him just like I had done while he was in the hospital. That way I could turn his assignments in with mine, and he'd pretty much stay up with all his assignments and not get any further behind.

"The only thing pressing this week is the book report we have to do over the book we read over vacation. Most of the classes we are doing nothing but reviewing so we can get ready for finals next week. Chris and I went over all the notes this afternoon when I got home."

"So, what have you done about the book report?"

"We typed out our rough drafts this afternoon so we're all set," Chris answered.

"Have you checked them over yet?" Doc asked.

"Not yet," I answered. "We thought we'd check each other's tomorrow and then go ahead and type the final drafts."

"Since there is nothing worth watching on TV tonight anyway, why don't you two check each other's papers over now and then write your second drafts. Then print them off and bring them out so I can take a look at them before you do your final drafts."

"Our second drafts?" I said somewhat stupidly. I had never written more than two copies of anything in my life, and I still managed to get mostly A's on compositions.

"Yes, your second drafts," Doc said with a slightly evil smile. "Unless, of course, you write that one to my satisfaction."

"Come on, Jason," Chris smirked. "We've got our work cut out for us tonight." He'd been through that routine before.

"Chris, there is no reason why we can't get our papers perfect on the second writing."

"Good luck," he said. "I've never been able to do it yet."

Talk about picky! I took my "perfect" paper out to him an hour later, and he massacred it. No English teacher ever glopped up one of my papers with the red ink the way he did.

"Jason, this isn't real good! I'm sure you can do better than this. Good writers do not write in what I call, 'Dick and Janese.' Every one of your sentences is a simple sentence. Look at the book you are reading and compare. You need to use a variety of different types of sentences and sentence lengths."

Ooops! So much for blowing through that assignment. With that ego boost, Doc took my book and pointed out sentence variety, action verbs used for description, original similes, and more. Yuck! He's supposed to be a doctor not an English teacher.

Finally, he just playfully swatted me across the butt with the book and grinned, "You're giving a really good analysis of your novel, but you've got to make it more exciting and fun to read. You do that by how you tell the story. However, enough is enough for tonight. Put it away and come out and watch the basketball game. Miami is getting clobbered by Detroit."

Thursday night I wrote my fourth and final draft. Doc liked it, I liked it, and hopefully my English teacher would like it. Doc was a perfectionist so all of our homework assignments had to be done the same way—perfectly.

One night after banging my head against the wall for two hours on a math assignment that was giving me fits, he made me recopy it because I had erased too many times and it was messy. He was always quizzing us on the stuff we had to do. He was more interested in our understanding the stuff than what our grade was going to be.

"What does this mean? How do you apply it? What is the author really saying?" I'm just glad he didn't see Chris and me rolling our eyes at each other when he started in on us.

My life had certainly changed for the better the past few weeks. There were guidelines and limits that I was expected to follow. The nicest part for me was the fact that they were consistent. They didn't change all the time. Since I knew what was expected of me, I was able to do it and not get into trouble. Life was good.

Chapter Ten

Chris went back to school the second week of January. That was finals week and school was only on half days. We took finals in the morning and the teachers had the afternoons to check them. His leg was still in a walking cast so he couldn't ride his bike. Therefore Mona took us every day and then picked us up after school What service!

Apparently the two of us were some kind of spectacle in the school and received a lot of attention from the kids and teachers alike. Whenever that happens some people take offense for some reason or the other. A group of kids that we referred to as hoods behind their backs suddenly decided they didn't like us. We had no clue what their problem was but decided to ignore them.

Some jerks just won't let you do that. After bouncing me into a locker, one of them asked, "How would you like to lose a couple of those pearly white teeth, Creep?"

"No thanks," I responded. "My dentist said they were all in good shape my last checkup."

"You're real wise," he snarled back. "If you weren't so gutless, you'd meet us at lunch time out behind the school. Then we'd see what great shape they're in as we splattered them onto the parking lot."

"Listen puke breath, If I could stand the suspension for fighting, I'd kick all three of your tails straight up between your shoulder blades here and now. However, I think I've been in enough trouble for one year all ready, so I guess I'll have to deny myself the pleasure this time." I've always had such a way with words.

"Boy, I've heard gutless excuses, but this one takes the cake," one of them mumbled as they walked away from us laughing under their breaths.

Nothing more was said until two days later when I met Chris by the door after school. I had gone to drop off our books in our locker and had left him alone for maybe five minutes at the most. When I came out the door, he was standing there dusting himself off. He was a mess.

"What happened to you?" I asked.

"Our friends decided that I needed a ride down the basement hallway. They knocked me down, grabbed my good leg, and dragged me down the hall on my back. When we reached the other end, they said to tell you that they would be free to 'discuss' it with you tomorrow during lunch behind the gym. I told them where they could stick it in no uncertain terms. We can't afford to lose any more school."

"I'll kill them! That's the lowest dirtiest thing I've ever seen. I'm gonna kill um!"

"Don't be stupid! There are three of them and only one of you because I can't help you out. Besides, if I'd know that you were going to completely lose your head, I never would have told you."

"Yes you would! I'd have hounded you until you told me what happened. Let me try to dust you off a little. Here comes Mona. Don't say anything. You take the back seat today and I'll take the front and maybe she won't notice."

We jumped into the car, and Mona didn't notice a thing. When we got home he went immediately to his room and changed clothes without even being told to for a change. That should have tipped her off big time that something was going on.

After changing Chris left our room as I stayed there plotting revenge. How would I handle three of them? I knew they wouldn't take me on one on one. This was going to be dirty.

I had to have some kind of weapon. If I could find something that I could hide maybe I could even up the odds just a bit. There was a broken broom handle in the garage that just might work. I sawed off a hunk about two feet long and took it back to our room. I was taping the handle when someone knocked on the door. It had to be Mona 'cause she and Doc were the only ones who knocked on the door when it was closed.

I slipped everything under the bed and opened the door. "May I come in?" she asked."

"Of course!" I answered as I stepped aside to let her in.

"Okay, young man. What's going on?" She asked as soon as she walked in, folded her arms, and glared at me.

"Why? What do you mean?"

"Every day you two jabber non-stop all the way home. Then you raid the cookie jar or whatever else I have around for you, and then you both come in here and do your homework. Today neither of you said one word to the other on the way home. When you got here, Chris changed his clothes without being told, came out to the living room, parked his fanny in a chair, and has stared a hole through the wall ever since. You barricaded yourself in here as soon as you got home, and neither one of you have been anywhere near the cookie jar that's full of still warm chocolate chip cookies. Chris won't say anything except to mumble under his breath when I ask him a question, so I guess you're elected. What is going on with you two?"

"It's not that big a deal. There's just this little problem at school that we have to work out, and we're both thinking about it."

"Is the problem between you two? Are you and Chris fighting?"

"No, no, no! We've never had a disagreement that lasted more than five seconds. We're fine."

"Well, that's good anyway. I don't want you two squabbling. So, what is the problem?"

"I just can't tell you right now. You'll just have to trust me. Everything will be ok."

"I'll take your word for it, but if I can help in any way, let me know."

Mona went back to the kitchen and more or less ignored both of us. After dinner I went back to our room, lay down on my bed, and stared at the ceiling thinking. Chris stayed away. I don't think he was real happy with me.

About seven thirty Doc yelled at me from the living room, "Jason, come out here!"

He never yelled and he sounded mad. They must have pumped it out of Chris.

As soon as I reached the living room, he started in on me, "Young man, fighting is stupid and has never solved anything. The idea of you taking on those three clowns single handedly is ridiculous!"

"Sir," I said clenching my jaw and staring him right in the eye," they've been bullying us ever since we got back to school for no reason except that they are jealous because of the attention we've gotten over the mess we got ourselves into. We've totally ignored them, but what they did to Chris today is the last straw. So help me, I'm gonna kill all three of them!"

"Don't you ever say that again!" he snapped. "You are not going to kill anyone, and I don't want you fighting either. I'll call the school tomorrow and get it settled once and for all."

"No!" I shouted. "Doc, please. Don't take away our self respect by treating us like babies. We can handle our own problems."

"Okay, I'll hold off calling the school for now, but I don't want you fighting those kids either."

"Is that an order, Sir?" I asked practically standing at attention.

"Quit calling me, 'Sir!' that way. I hate that. Besides, what's the difference whether I'm asking you or telling you, either way, I don't want you fighting."

"Because either way I can't promise that I'll obey you. I can't promise anything right now."

"Jason, I'm hedging and I know it. That's why I don't want to demand anything. I know that sometimes a person has to do what he thinks is right regardless of the consequences. If I make it an order for you not to fight, and you do it anyway, we both lose. I lose because you will force me into doing something I don't want to do, and you lose because you're the one who will be punished severely. Do you understand what I'm saying?"

"Dad!" Chris screamed. "You can't threaten to punish him for something like this. It's not fair!"

"Shut up, Chris!" Doc and I said in unison as we stared at each other. If tensions hadn't been so high, it would have been funny.

Finally with a deep sigh I looked over at Chris, "Stay out of it. This is between doc and me now. Doc, may I go back to my room?"

"Yes, maybe that's a good idea. Let's both think this over for awhile before we make any rash decisions that we're both forced to live with. Before you go to bed I want us to talk again. I don't want you to go to sleep with this hanging in the air."

I went to my room and lay down on the bed and stared at the ceiling. Doc was right about one thing anyway, I didn't want to go to sleep with this hanging over my head. Finally I made a decision. I took off my belt and laid it over the end of the bed. Then I went to the door and called Doc, "Could you come in here for a minute, please?"

When I heard the evening paper rustle as he got out of his easy chair, I closed the door and walked over to the bed. I lay down over the end of it, folded my arms under my head, and waited.

Doc walked into the room and stopped dead in his tracks. After a second or two he closed the door and walked over to me. "What's going on?" he asked. "Just what exactly is going on?"

"Doc, listen to me. I don't know for sure what is going to happen tomorrow, but I'm guessing there's gonna be one big brawl. I've got enough to worry about as it is trying to figure out how I'm going to handle all three of them at the same time. I know they won't fight fair. Tomorrow's going to be a disaster all day. All morning long I'll be thinking about this so school will be a lost cause. I won't learn a thing. Then at lunch time if I meet them I'll probably get the crap knocked out of me. Then the principal will drag all of us into the office and we'll get kicked out of school for awhile under their zero tolerance for fighting policy. Then you or Mona will come and get me, I'll get yelled at all the way home, and then you'll drag me in here and beat my butt until my back teeth rattle."

"That was quite a speech. So what's your point? Why are you lying there with your belt off and lying beside you?"

"I don't want this on my mind until tomorrow because it won't make any difference. So, please, grab the belt and just beat me with it and get it over with. That way I can just concentrate on those three idiots I have to face tomorrow."

"I couldn't see him, but there was a change in the one of his voice, "Suppose by chance things worked out so you didn't have to fight tomorrow. Then what? You would have been spanked for nothing and that's not fair either."

"If that happened, we could just figure that you owe me one. Some time down the road when I get in another scrape and you get really mad at me, you could let me go scot free and we'd be even."

"You doof," he said. "turn around here and sit up so we can talk." When I did, he grabbed a hold of me and hugged me. "I am not going to beat you with a belt now or ever." Then he arched his eyebrows and said smiling, "Which doesn't mean I won't warm the seat of your pants for you, but I'll use my hand and never a belt. In the meantime, I don't want you getting hurt by three kids ganging up on you. What can I do to help?"

"Just support me, Doc. Wish me the best of luck, and we can both hope that everything turns out okay. I don't want to get hurt either, but sometimes, like you said, we all have to make hard decision in life and live by the consequences."

We talked for quite awhile before he left. As soon as he walked out, I took the broom handle out of hiding and threw it in the closet. At least that was one decision that I felt I could live with. No weapons. I don't know when Chris came to bed, because I crawled under the covers and fell asleep almost immediately.

School the next day was tough. Trying to concentrate on my classes was a real picnic. It was a long time until lunch. When the bell finally rang I headed out the gym door and there they were along with a whole slew of their friends who came along to watch the show. I hadn't told anyone—even Chris exactly where or when so he wasn't even there for encouragement. The three of them started circling me like a pack of wild dogs, and I just flipped out.

The whole thing made me so mad that I guess I lost it completely. Some of the kids told me later that I just started flailing like a mad man. I really don't remember a thing until someone grabbed me and literally picked me up off the ground and held me in the air yelling in my ear to calm down.

When we landed in the principal's office all four of us were filthy from rolling on the ground, bloody, and badly bruised and scraped up. I didn't feel a thing. Adrenalin was still surging big time. After he called our parents and told them to come and get us, the three of them started blaming each other for the whole thing and I didn't have to say a word. It was great! They pretty much cleared me of all blame except for defending myself.

When Doc arrived punishments had all ready been handed out. They were suspended for three days and I was to be sent home for the rest of the day. He told the parents he was leaving any other punishments up to them.

"I'm really disappointed that Jason allowed himself to get sucked into this fracas, and I intend to discuss it further when we get home. We talked about all his options last night for two hours and the final decision was his so he has to pay the consequences for making what I consider a poor choice," Doc said giving me a look that made me cringe. I was in dog poop up to my arm pits.

When we left the school we went directly to his office where he marched me right through the front door and the waiting room instead of taking me in the back door like normal. "Is the sound proof examining room available, Marge?" he asked the receptionist loud enough for everyone in the place to hear.

The horrified look on my face caught her attention because as soon as he headed for the door, she smiled at me and winked— as if maybe he wasn't serious. I sure hoped not.

When we got to the examining room, which was just a regular room, he said, "Strip down to your boxers and sit up on the examining table and wait. I'm calling Mona to come pick you up. I have a couple of things to do, and then I'll be back."

In about two minutes he was back and started checking me

over to see if I needed stitches or anything else. He checked my nose to make sure it wasn't broken, the cuts over my eyes, and my teeth to make sure nothing was loose.

When he finished smearing on anti septic, zapping in two stitches on my eye brow, and other patching, he stood in from of me and let me have it, "You are grounded for one week starting now and ending a week from tomorrow morning when your alarm goes off. There will be no friends, telephone calls, emails, text messages, television, computer games, or IPod during this time. Am I clear?"

"Can I breathe?" Oh, no! I can't believe I really said that. "Doc, I'm sorry. I really am. That just slipped out."

"Ok, but give me your cell phone and IPod and then get back up on the table until Mona gets here. She should be any minute now. I have to go help out my assistants with a couple of patients."

It wasn't five minutes later that Mona walked in. She didn't act overly glad to see me either. "What am I going to do with you, young man?" she asked as she grabbed a wash cloth and started giving me a sponge bath right there on the table.

"I'm grounded for a week. That's an awful long time," I whined. "I've never been grounded before and I'm not sure how to act. My dad always just beat up on me and then it was over until next time."

"I know. Doc and I talked it over on the phone and figured that was an appropriate amount. You'll have plenty of time to think about the decision you made against our wishes. In the meantime, nobody is going to 'beat up' on you. You're going to be in enough pain from all the bruises you received in your little back alley scrap you got yourself into today."

"Things are starting to hurt all ready. I feel really achy and sore all over."

"Not surprised. Now get dressed and we'll go home and you can get into the shower and wash your hair and get rid of the rest of the dirt that I missed."

The next week was the longest week of my life. I wouldn't talk to anyone at school, even Chris. I ate my lunch at the school's detention table so no one could talk to me. All the kids knew the situation and cooperated by leaving me alone. I was an outcast.

Sunday night after we cleaned up the table after dinner, I asked Doc to come to our room. "Doc, won't you please just take a belt and whip me and get it over? I can't handle three more days. This is killing me!"

He grabbed a hold of me and hugged me tightly, "You know I love you. I consider you my son, and I try to treat you like you are. I would not whip you with a belt under any circumstances. Believe it or not, this is not hard on only you. The rest of us are suffering under the silent treatment as well. Thursday morning your time will be up. We will all live with it until then."

With that he gave me another quick squeeze and walked out of the room. Dang! Puberty did me in again.

When I got up Thursday morning and went out to breakfast, my cell phone and IPod were sitting at my place at the table. The longest week of my life was over.

Chapter Eleven

That spring had to be one of the happiest periods of my life. Everything went right. There were no more problems at school, Chris kissed the cast goodbye a week early, and both of us had great report cards. He had all A's and I had all A's and one B. The strange part was for the first time in my life I was nervous about taking home a report card. Two weeks into March I had a bout of the flu over the weekend. I should have stayed home Monday, but I had missed so much school earlier, I didn't want to be out if I could help it. Doc wanted me to stay home, but he didn't insist. He said I wouldn't hurt myself going, but I wouldn't be at my best either.

Our science teacher popped a sneak quiz on us that Monday, and I bombed it. That one test dropped me from an A to a B+, and that was the class that Doc emphasized most.

"What's Doc going to say about that B?" I asked Chris as we were pedaling home on our bikes.

"He'll probably yell at you for a half hour, beat you, and then ground you until summer vacation"

There were times when Chris was just the biggest help. Doc was a stickler about school, but at least he wasn't that bad. I hoped.

When we got home, we gave our cards to Mona and started right in on our homework. We were just finishing up when he pulled into the driveway.

He wasn't in the house five minutes when we heard him call us, "Jason!...Chris!...Front and center!"

We hustled into the living room. Mona winked at us and smiled and then headed out to the kitchen to finish dinner. "What a ham!" she said shaking her head.

"Why aren't there any ones in citizenship this time? Don't you guys realize that the way you behave in school is just as important as your grades?"

"Aw, Dad," Chris said, "Unless you're terrible, all the teachers just mark everyone with a blanket two. The only people who get ones are the 'goodie goodies' and those are always girls."

"I don't buy that," he answered. "I hadn't planned on going to conferences with your mom tonight, but I guess maybe I'd better. Just perhaps you two are goofing around a little too much in class? Don't get me wrong, your grades are fine—even though I do expect a certain B+ to end up as an A when final grades come out. I am concerned about those citizenship marks."

Sure enough, at seven o'clock Doc and Mona headed out the door for parent-teacher conferences. Fortunately, we both were given good reports from all our teachers so were off the hook.

Mona and Doc were consistent. They accepted nothing but our best at all times. They understood the B because I had warned them in advance about trashing that one test when I should have stayed home. We might have even been able to get away with two or three B's between us on our cards, but we better not bring home a C or a 3 in citizenship, or they would have taken turns skinning us alive.

My blood parents never even looked at my report cards. They were always ok—nothing stellar, and one of them would just sign them and I would take them back. Occasionally, he'd ask how I was doing, and I'd tell him. That's all there would be to it. Personally, I don't think he gave a rip what I did in school.

Say what you want, it does make a difference when someone is concerned about you and actually cares how you are doing. I worked very hard to hear Mona and Doc tell me that they were proud of me.

Even though I was technically a foster child and ward of the court, I didn't feel like it. They showed no favoritism. Chris belonged to a teen book club so they signed me up. The day my first book came in the mail was exciting for several reasons.

"Mona, I'm home!" I yelled out when I walked in the door. Chris had stayed after school to check on some assignment so I came on home. I was hungry. There was a note on the counter,

> Boys,
> I've gone down town shopping—be back around four. Save some of the cake for desert tonight, and don't spoil your dinners!! Someone check the mail,
> Love

First things first! I cut a huge piece of cake. It was my favorite kind, German Chocolate. I wasn't going to wait for Chris to come home this time. Mona was always worried about us spoiling our appetites for dinner, and we never did. The only thing that was spoiled around there was Chris and me. She baked something almost every day, "Just to tide you two over until dinner."

I think if either one of us ever came home from school and said we weren't hungry, she'd be heartbroken. I know Doc would have a thermometer in our mouths within five minutes.

After eating about half my cake and my first glass of milk, I decided I'd better check the mail before I forgot.

"All Right!" I yelled when I reached into the box and pulled out my new book with the rest of the mail. I had ordered it through the book club on line just a few days ago and was all excited.

Tried to tear the tape off and it wouldn't budge. Good grief! Nothing like using steel tape. I knew there was a carton cutter on the shelf in the garage so I set the package down and went out and got it. That should work perfectly, I thought. The blade looked a bit jagged and rusty, but that didn't matter.

Well, it did. It pulled hard through the tape so I just reefed on it. Wonderful! The blade slipped and came up my left thumb and across my wrist.

"Ow! Crap! Crap! Crap!" I yelled as the blood spurted out of my wrist. The first gusher hit my milk glass, cake, and the counter all at the same time.

I grabbed my wrist with my right hand and that only slowed things down a little bit. Blood was still squirting out all over the place.

"Think, Stupid. Think!" I said to myself trying to calm down so I could use my head just a little. Wet compress! I had heard that someplace. I grabbed the dish towel, soaked it in water and wrapped it as tightly as I could around my wrist.

By that time the place was a gory mess. There was blood all over the kitchen. I had to get to Doc's office fast. Somebody would be there even if he didn't happen to be. Would he be in the office? Was it his day for rounds at the hospital? I didn't have a clue. I wasn't thinking real clearly.

His office was a mile away, but I could get there fast on my bike. I jumped on and headed out holding my wrist as tightly as I could against my belly. I held the handle bar with my right hand. I felt a little light headed but figured that was just because I was kind of shook up. When I got to his office I just dropped my bike on the sidewalk in front of the door and barged in. It probably would have been a little classier to slip in the back door and not scare all the patients waiting in the lobby, but I was scared to death and not thinking too clearly. As I stumbled across the reception room, I heard people sucking air all over the place. When I had a chance to check myself over later, I could see why. My shirt and pants were literally soaked from the waist down.

I went right up to the window and blurted out, "Marge, I've got to see Doc. Now!"

"Jason, what's the matter? You look like you've seen a ghost."

All she could see was my face and upper body so I stepped back so she could get a good look. "I cut myself. I think it might be bad."

She jumped up out of her seat and ran to the door, "Get in here!" she said sharply.

The head nurse was about ten feet away and perked up when she heard the tone of Marge's voice. She was there instantly. "Where are you cut?" she asked. You couldn't tell by looking at me.

"My wrist," I told her.

She grabbed my arm about six inches above the cut and squeezed. The flow of blood slowed to a trickle almost immediately. "Come with me," she said leading me down the hall and not letting up on the pressure. "Marge, would you tell Jack that we have an emergency?"

Doc was with a patient when Marge banged on his door, "Dr. Jackson, we seem to have an emergency. Jason's in room two. He cut his wrist and is bleeding like a stuck hog."

Doc excused himself from his patient and rushed in. "Looks like we have a little problem here. How did you manage this?"

"My new book came in the mail today," I told him. "I couldn't break the tape, so I used a box cutter on it. The darned thing slipped and caught my thumb and wrist."

The nurse raced in and out several times bringing more and more junk. Doc scrubbed out the cut with something that felt like a toothbrush, and I thought I would go through the ceiling. I knew he had to be punishing me for interrupting his office routine for the afternoon. Suddenly, the nurse slipped him a hypo that looked like it was fresh out of a Frankenstein movie.

"Jason," he said, "I want you to relax your arm as much as possible and look out the window. This is going to sting a little."

No way it could hurt as much as it did when he scrubbed it out so I asked him, "Why? I want to watch. Besides, what are you going to do with that horse needle?"

"Suit yourself," he answered ignoring my question. However, it won't hurt so much if you don't watch."

He took the hypo and started stabbing my arm all around the cut. I thought he was making holes for the stitches and asked him why he had to do that.

He and the nurse both laughed at me over that one, but I was still nervous about what he was doing. "I'm just numbing your arm so it won't hurt when I put in the stitches," he said.

At that point I decided that I'd seen enough and looked out the window like he told me to do in the first place. I could feel the pressure of him tugging on the stitches, but it didn't hurt anymore.

After he finished I started to watch what he was doing again. He painted my wrist and thumb with some kind of red gunk and then held my arm out until it dried.

About that time Marge stuck her head in the door again, "Dr. Jackson, Mona is on line two."

"Oh, no!" I cried out suddenly remembering the kitchen.

"What's the matter?" Doc asked looking at me.

"Mona is going to kill me. There's blood all over the kitchen, and I didn't stop to clean it up. Tell her I'm sorry, and that I'll clean it up when I get home."

"I'm not going to do your dirty work for you," he said with a grin. "You're going to have to do your own plea bargaining with her. However, I kind of doubt that she's too angry with you."

With that he flipped the switch on the speaker phone and answered. She sounded pretty shook up when she spoke, "Jack, have you seen anything of either one of the boys? Someone has been hurt badly in the kitchen. There's blood all over the counter and the floor."

"Jason slashed his thumb and wrist on a carton cutter trying to open his new book. He's here now. I just finished putting in about twenty stitches—more or less. He's going to be fine, a bit sore, but fine."

"Thank heavens for that!" she said sounding a little bit more relieved.

"Mona," I cut in, "I'm sorry about the blood all over everything. I'll clean it up when I get home."

"Don't you worry about that, Honey, are you doing okay?"

"Yeah, sure! Doc fixed me all up and I'll be as good as new."

"Jack, do you want me to come pick Jason up or do you want him to wait there until you leave?"

"I'll be okay," I cut in. "I can just ride my bike home."

"Yes," doc answered, "come and get him. I'm going to be a bit later this afternoon, and he is not riding his bike home. I'll just throw it in the trunk when I leave and bring it with me. All we need now is to have him pass out because of the blood loss and fall on his face in front of a car.

"Incidentally, bring a change of clothes and a plastic garbage bag for the stuff he has on. Everything is ruined and can be trashed."

"How complete a change does he need?"

"Everything! Shirt, pants, underwear, socks, and shoes. Believe me, he's a mess."

"Ok, I'll be there just as quickly as I can."

Doc had his nurse bandage me up so he could go back to the patient he had been dealing with when this all started. Before she left the room, she told me to strip down completely, wrap a towel around my waist, and clean up the best I could while I was waiting for Mona and my clean clothes. She gave me a towel, wash cloth, and a bar of soap and filled the basin with hot water.

A few minutes later Doc came in hiding something behind his back. So far, I had washed my face and combed my hair.

"What are you hiding, Doc?" I asked trying to see around behind him.

He gave me an evil, devilish look and said, "It's a hypo eighteen inches long that I'm going to stab you with."

I immediately started backing away with a panicked look on my face.

"It's just a regular hypo with a tetanus vaccine and a few anti-biotics thrown in for good measure. It'll sting a little bit, but it's not nearly as bad a deal it would be if you came down with lock jaw. Now, turn around. Normally, I'd give this to you in the arm, but this way we can hide the red mark." Then he laughed and messed up my hair for me.

All I had on was the towel wrapped around me that the nurse had brought. He lifted the edge of the thing and nailed me. He might have been joking about the eighteen inch needle, but that's what it felt like. After that, he left again and I went back to my hair. I just couldn't get it the way I wanted it.

A few minutes later Doc and Mona walked in together. She had my clean clothes and set them down on the examining table.

"If he's through combing his hair, why don't you give him a hand cleaning up. At the rate he's going, it'll be his bed time before he finishes. Here he is all covered with blood, and so far, he's spent ten minutes on his hair. I'll be back after my next patient to see how things are going. And, oh, somewhere along the line we probably need to have a discussion about eleven year olds using dangerous tools unsupervised by an adult. Also, we might want to work on memorizing the phone number for 911 in case we ever need it again. Riding your bike with your wrist gushing blood is not exactly the wisest thing to do that I can think of."

We did not need to have that discussion, but I knew we would. Seems like I have to learn everything the hard way.

Mona grabbed the soap and washcloth and in five minutes time gave me a full-fledged sponge bath—including my face again which I figured I'd done a pretty good job on—while I stood there. I felt a little embarrassed standing there naked as a jay bird after she pulled off the towel, but it didn't faze her one bit. "This is the second time we've done this in the past couple of months. Is my bathing you at the doctor's office becoming some kind of a habit?"

"I hope not", I said grinning rather sheepishly. "Especially, since last time I got grounded for a week."

"That's not going to happen this time," she continued. "Has anyone told you that you're an absolute mess? Dried blood is very sticky so we've going to scrub it off of you this way even if you aren't too happy about it. You probably won't be able to take a shower today."

"I know," I said. I swore she was using a scrub pad on me.

By that time the shot was working well, and the inflammation on my hip was quite noticeable.

"What happened here" she asked.

"Oh, that?" I said very innocently and straight faced when I saw what she was looking at. "Doc did that a little while ago."

"How?"

"I think he's a pit peeved at me for disrupting his schedule. He came in while I was combing my hair, pulled back the towel, and let me have it on the butt. Then he said, 'There, that ought to take care of you!' and then he left."

"No, he didn't!" she said with a tone of voice that didn't sound right.

"No, I'm just kidding," I told her. I didn't want her to go after him in a huff, and she acted like she just might.

"It was a tetanus shot."

"Oh, you," she sputtered and playfully gave me a little backhanded swat on the other side.

By the time Doc was finished with his next patient, I was dressed and ready to go.

"Chris called and was all shaken up," he said when he came in. "You must have left quite a mess."

"I did and I'll clean it up as soon as we get home."

"Oh, no you won't. When you get home you are to drink some juice and then go lie down on your bed and take a look at that new book that caused all of this. You've lost a lot of blood—more than your realize. You're pretty lucky you didn't pass out on the way. So, listen up. Doctor's orders. No shower until tomorrow morning. You might feel a little sticky even after Mona cleaned you up, but you'll live. I don't want you passing out in the hot water and drowning yourself," he smiled and messed up my hair again.

"Secondly, I want you on your bed until I get home. You don't have to sleep if you don't feel like it, but I do want you down and resting. We'll see how you're doing when I get there."

You should have seen the looks Mona and I got when we walked back through the waiting room. My episode had thrown the office schedule about a half hour behind. Most of the people there had been there when I stumbled in. Surprisingly, no one looked too hostile; in fact some even appeared to be a little sympathetic.

When we got home, I went straight to the kitchen to inspect the mess. It was clean. When Chris found out what had happened, he took care of the gore. Some of the stains hadn't come out of the throw rug in front of the sink, but Mona said she'd throw it in the washing machine and it would be fine.

She poured a huge glass of Cranberry-Raspberry juice and then shooed me off to bed with Chris in tow. He wanted all the gory details before he went off to finish his homework.

"Chris, I owe you one for cleaning up that mess. Thanks!"

"Forget it. I had to do something while I waited for you to come home and I couldn't concentrate on school work so I just cleaned it up. Somebody had to," he grinned. "Now I'm going to go down to the family room and try to get my algebra done before I forget what he told me when I went in after school."

I kicked off my shoes and grabbed my new book and opened it. Figured I'd get a long ways. I was still wired and knew that I had the rest of the afternoon to lie there with nothing else to do.

I made it a long way all right. I made it all the way to page two. A little after six Doc walked in, "Are you going to sleep all day or come have dinner with the rest of us?"

I smiled and crawled out of bed. I was starved.

Fortunately, my wrist and thumb healed quickly, and everything was back to normal. Life was great and I was as happy as if I were in my right mind. However, towards the end of May, my whole world came crashing down.

Chapter Twelve

Probate Court sent a letter the last week of May. They scheduled a meeting on the sixth of June in the Judge's chambers. No one had to tell me what it was all about. My old man had sweet talked some psychologist or psychiatrist into saying he was cured so I'd have to go to Michigan.

Having his son taken away because of his tendency towards child abuse must have been a real embarrassment to him. Those things just shouldn't happen to an attorney. People might look down their noses at him. Horrors! Of course, when you had a rotten son like he had, those things happened. Just ask him.

After reading the letter I went to my room, locked the door, and threw myself on the bed. I had the most delightful conniption fit I could throw. It was the closest thing to a full-fledged temper tantrum I ever had. Chris and Mona both tried to get in to talk to me, but I wouldn't unlock the door. I just lay there and stomped my feet up and down and bawled like a two year old. This was not puberty in action, I was mad.

Doc came home at the usual time, and as I had predicted to myself, within five minutes he was at the door.

"Jason, open up and let me in. I want to talk to you," he called through the door.

By then I had calmed down somewhat so I unlocked the door and let him in. I grabbed a hold of him and pleaded, "Doc, please don't make me go. I don't want to. For the first time in my life I'm happy. Why can't those people just leave me alone?"

When I looked up, doc had tears in his eyes, "I sure as the devil don't want you to go either. How do you think I feel? I signed that stupid agreement saying he could have you back if he met certain conditions believing he never would bother. Anyway, maybe we're jumping to conclusions. Maybe the judge is just checking up on us to see how many times a week I have to beat you to keep you in line."

We both kind of half heartedly laughed over that one. In all that time Doc had never laid a hand on me. However, I knew in my heart that this was the beginning of the end. Blood is thicker than water in the eyes of the law, and I knew they were going to send me to Michigan. The fact that I had been deliriously happy for the past seven months in a family where we all loved and cared for one another was irrelevant. According to all the experts, a child should be with his natural parents whenever possible.

Our worst fears were realized the next week in the judge's chamber. He had received correspondence from a Lansing, Michigan psychologist stating that my father had been successfully treated for his drinking and abusive tendencies and was considered cured. It was his professional opinion that I should be reunited with my family immediately. All that without ever talking to me.

Having no alternative, the judge ordered that I be sent to Michigan the Monday following the last day of school. That spring might have been the happiest period of my life, but those last two weeks had to be the gloomiest.

Monday, June 12th arrived. Chris and I got up at the normal time for breakfast and barely said a word to each other. It seemed that all I did was look at the clock. My plane was scheduled to leave Tampa International Airport at two p.m. Doc took the day off to take me. He was antsy too. He paced the house without talking too. He started to read the paper, but couldn't pay any attention to that either. The atmosphere around there was getting to me so I said to Chris, "Why don't you help me check to see if I packed everything?"

He looked at me kind of funny because he had helped me pack everything the night before and we had double checked the list Mona had given us a couple of times. He didn't argue though, he just headed down the hall to our bed room.

He sat down on his bed and folded his legs Indian style. "So, what's on your mind?" he asked.

"Let's move your bed back in here from the guest room and take the twins back there. There's nothing else to do for a while so I might just as well help you. Besides, it will kill some time before I have to leave."

Chris had a puzzled look on his face when he asked, "What for? Why should we screw up our room? Besides, I like it this way."

"I just figured you'd move the furniture around like it was before I came. It only seems fair that I help."

"Yeah, sure! Then we'll just have to move it all back when you haul your dumb butt back here. That would be kind of stupid, wouldn't it?"

"You heard the judge. I'm not coming back. This is forever."

"Bull! Forever is a long time. Somehow, some way, you'll be back, and I don't mean just for a visit. Don't ask me how I know, because I don't. But ever since that letter came, I've had this feeling in my gut. So there isn't any reason to move the stuff all around.

Oh, by the way, I'm not going to the airport with you this

afternoon. I'm not going to make a complete fool out of myself in public if I can help it. I'll just say goodbye to you when you leave, and then I'll see you again when you come back.

That was okay with me. I understood perfectly. A big spectacle at the airport wouldn't do either one of us any good. Leaving was hard enough as it was. I just wished I had the confidence that Chris had that I was coming back. It wouldn't seem so much like doomsday.

About 11:30 Mona came down with a migraine headache. Like Chris, that was her way of saying she didn't want any part of the airport scene. I couldn't blame her. I didn't want any part of it either.

Around noon doc and I loaded the car and were ready to go. I said my sloppy goodbyes to Mona and then looked around for Chris. He had split. Not only wouldn't he go to the airport, he wouldn't even say goodbye. Good. I didn't want to either.

Doc was great. When I tried to give him back my cell phone, he told me, "No, you keep it. We have unlimited family minutes. Call any time for any reason. Keep us all posted on what you are doing, what's going on, whatever, just make sure you keep in touch and keep the battery charged."

He chattered non-stop all the way to the airport. After we checked in, he bought me lunch. I wasn't very hungry and neither was he. When they called my flight number, we raced down to the boarding area. As I was getting ready to go through that final door, he hugged me and kissed my cheek. Without a word, he spun a 180 on his heal and headed the other way. I knew why. He was doing the same thing I was. I could hardly see to get on the plane.

At 2:05 the big jet that I was on lifted off the runway and roared skyward. My stomach flip-flopped so I dug out the Dramamine that Doc had given me before I left. Then I looked out over Tampa Bay for the last time. I was leaving the place I loved for Michigan, the Water wonderland.

A couple of hours later I understood the state's logo. Cloud to cloud lightening chased the plane all over the sky. That was all I needed—fly some idiot plane for a thousand miles and then crash. We circled Detroit Metro for an hour and a half before the storm cleared so we could start our descent. At five-thirty we touched down. My parents had decided to pick me up in Detroit instead of my waiting three hours for a connecting flight to Lansing. I wondered if they would actually be there to meet me or would I have to find my own way to Lansing.

Sure enough, as I ambled into the terminal, there they were. Both had big grins on their faces as we walked towards each other. Mom gave me a big kiss right there in front of everyone, and Dad grabbed my hand. The big show embarrassed me, but at least we were off to a good start.

The airport restaurant looked relatively empty so we decided to eat dinner there. Food hadn't interested me all day so I was starved by then. By eight-thirty we were on I=94 headed 100 miles west towards Lansing, my new home.

The house was old but okay. It was located on the east side of town about two miles from the capitol building. Sparrow Hospital was only a couple of blocks from our house. It would have been ideal for Doc. I would be in the eighth grade in September so I would go to the brand new Pattengil Middle School. At least that was one plus to this whole thing.

My school in Florida was a little on the old side, but I really hadn't ever paid much attention. We had great teachers there, and I imagined I would have the same thing in the new school. At this point in time, I really didn't care.

Tuesday morning I hopped on my bike and explored the area around home. I discovered Hunter's park a short distance away.

There were tennis courts, ball diamonds, a green house, and picnic tables. But the biggest attraction was the pool nestled in a little wooded area. The pool turned out to be a lot of fun, but it was awkward to get to. I had to either walk or ride my bike down this one street. It was called Clifford Street, and it always gave me the willies. The street was lined on both sides with retirees who sat on their porches and glared at me over the tops of their magazines or newspapers. My use of their sidewalks or street apparently violated their serenity. Our feelings for each other were mutual. They didn't' trust me and I didn't trust them. Too bad we couldn't have somehow gotten to know one another.

Mom had checked on the pool hours in advance so I took my suit with me on Wednesday for the first time. There was a line up at the gate waiting to get in. The conglomeration of people amused me. There were blacks, whites, yellows, reds, and everything in between—all ages, and both sexes. A good photographer would have had a field day.

A sharp jab in the ribs as I stood in line bought be to my senses, "You buying today, Kid?" asked the boy who was standing behind me in line. He was about my age and size, but he didn't have my Florida sun tan. He looked kind of pale and sickly.

"Huh?" I asked real intelligent like. "What are you talking about?"

"Are you looking for a little pot today? I've got some for sale if you need it," he answered looking down his nose at me as if I were really kind of stupid for asking.

"No, no thanks," I answered. "I'm all set."

I was all set ok. I didn't want any of that junk. What shocked me was how out in the open that kid was. He just came out and asked me if I wanted to buy drugs. Not at all shy. I suppose that's what it takes to be a good salesman. You have to be a bit on the brash side.

My first day at the pool wasn't' all that much fun. I didn't know a soul there so it was kind of boring. Decided it would be a good time to call Chris. Sat on one of the deck chairs and pulled out my phone. Ended up calling all three Jacksons. It seemed so good to hear their voices. Gone two days and I was homesick.

Dinner that night was catch as catch can. I was on my own. Mom and Dad were going to some dinner club they belonged to so I had to check out the leftovers. I was glad to see I wasn't going to cramp their style of living at all, especially on my second full day home. That would have been mighty selfish on my part if I do say so myself. I hadn't eaten all by myself in seven months, and I wasn't particularly happy about doing it then.

After eating I didn't have anything better to do so I rode my bike out to The Shopping Center, a shopping mall on the eastern city limits. There was every kind of store you could think of so it was fun browsing and day dreaming about all the stuff I would love to have. There was a big drug store on one corner of the mall so I wandered in. Still hungry from my crumby two hot dog dinner, I bought a couple of candy bars. Then I checked out the rest of the place. The Shopping Center closed at nine so that's when I left.

Heading out of the mall, I spotted lights to the east so I went to see what that was all about. A city soft ball game was in progress so I watched that for awhile.

An hour later I was getting tired so I headed home. My parents were there waiting for me when I walked into the house.

"Where have you been?" Dad asked. "We've been worried about you out running around a town you know nothing about until late."

He wasn't terribly impressed when I told him.

"I don't like the idea of you spending too much time at the mall," he told me. "The way you have a tendency to get yourself into trouble, you might get picked up for shop lifting or something."

"Thanks a lot! You've really got a lot of confidence in me haven't you?"

"I just don't want you getting into any trouble. I have a new job I need to protect and don't need you screwing things up for me. You've been a big enough slur on the family name as it is."

"Bite me!" I screamed and stomped out of the room.

He was on me like stink on a skunk, "don't press your luck, young man! I don't know how you talked to the Jacksons, but you aren't going to talk to me that way. Do you understand?"

"I sure do! None of them ever called me a thief. None of them ever gave me a reason to yell back!"

Nothing had changed. Dad and I had been separated all that time, and we still couldn't get along. At least he didn't hit me. Maybe the counseling had done him some good after all.

Totally disgusted I went to my room and immediately jumped on my computer and Emailed Chris. I told him everything.

Then I went to bed and just lay there stewing about the situation. Finally, I came to a decision. If he were going to be a total jerk to me, maybe I should be one too. It was time to start planning my escape out of that place. There was no way I was staying until I got out of school.

As I lay there in bed I remembered a story Doc told us one night at dinner that one of his cop buddies had told him that day. There was this kid who stole like the Thief of Bagdad. He pawned everything he stole and invested the money in stocks and bonds. That kid was worth over fifty thousand dollars before he hit his teens. He apparently came from a crappy home and some adult took him under his wing and helped him invest the money in his name since he couldn't do it on his own.

The cops knew what he was doing and how he was doing it,

but they couldn't catch him or his accomplice in the act. Talk about a predicament! If they actually caught him and put him away until he was nineteen, that money would just sit there and grow in value. They couldn't touch that with a ten foot pole and they knew it.

I couldn't work a scam like that because I had no adult around to help me, but I bet I was smart enough to steal a ton of stuff and get away with it.

Decision time! If dear old dad wanted to accuse me of being a thief, I'd show him just what the kid could do. I would spend the next sixty day stealing everything of value that I could lay my hands on. I would keep a journal as to what I took, when, and where. At the end of the sixty days, I'd arrange it to get caught—show everyone what I had accomplished—turn over all the loot—humiliate the old man—and head off to the juvenile home until I was eighteen. If that is what he expected out of me, that is what he would get.

Chapter Thirteen

If I were going to spend the next sixty days becoming Lansing's resident thief, I had to get started. The next morning I rode my bike out to The Shopping Center to the book store and bought a journal. Probably should have stolen it, but didn't think of it at the time.

Went home and checked out the surroundings. The garage had a trap door leading to the storage area above. There was a ladder on the wall so I pulled it down and checked out the area above. Perfect! It was an ideal cache. Mom would never have a reason to go up there as it was all ready empty, and the fat man couldn't. Ta Da! I was all set.

That afternoon I headed back out to the shopping center. My first successful acquisition was a Precious Moments figurine from a gift store. The stupid looking thing had absolutely no value to me what so ever. However, it cost a lot of money so at least some people apparently liked them. I took it home and tagged it No. 1 with a sticker and then logged it in my journal. I put down the store, the price, and the date. I was off to a great start.

Brass book ends and a fifty dollar pen and pencil set were my conquests the following day. Every single item I took was valued at twenty dollars or more, strictly non-perishable, and treated very carefully. I didn't want to damage anything and then have to pay for it in the end. I figured that the store owners would have to be happy to get their merchandise back or it would be a wasted effort. The first week alone I stole over five-hundred dollars worth. The game was fun.

I emailed Chris every day and Doc or Mona a couple times a week. Obviously I didn't tell them what I was doing. I told them about going to the ball games, checking out my new school that I would be going to in September, my run ins with my dad which were on going, and everything else except my "game."

Chris's emails were fun. He wrote like he talked. I could just hear him saying the things he wrote just like we were sitting on our beds talking like we used to do.

Doc and Chris had gone fishing out in the Gulf. They hadn't caught anything but sunburn, but it had been a great day. They both told me all about that. Wish I had been there with them. Doc was spending a lot more time with Chris these days.

Mona wrote me a long email. When I had talked to her earlier that day on our cell phones, she thought she had picked up a tone in my voice that indicated I was pretty depressed. She was worried about me. I was going to have to be more careful. I tried to keep everything light when I talked to her and Doc. If she had any clue as to what was going on, she'd have a stroke. The only one I told how I really felt was Chris.

Their emails and phone calls made me horribly homesick. There was no way under the sun that I would ever pull the stunt I was pulling now if I were still with them. I guess that is why I felt so guilty. I felt as if I were letting them down. They were the best people in the whole world. I could care less about letting my parents down. That really was part of the plan.

Saturday night I was still up watching the late show when Mom and Dad staggered in. They had gone out to dinner with some friends for the fourth night out of the last seven.

Wonderful! I thought to myself. This should be the acid test. They're both stewed to the gills.

Dad was his normal bitchy self when he had been drinking. "What are you doing still up?" he belched. "You should have been in bed hours ago."

As he turned off the television, he turned to my mom, "That brat thinks he can get away with anything he wants. I've got a good notion to show him what he can get away with and what he can't right here and now."

"Oh, Honey," she said. "It wouldn't do any good and you know it. Let's just go to bed ourselves and forget about him for tonight. I don't feel very well."

"Okay, this time!" he said glaring at me.

I headed down the hallway ahead of him before he changed his mind. As I turned the handle and started to open the bedroom door, he drove me through the open doorway with the side of his foot to my hind end. It was like a regular soccer style field goal attempt. It felt so good! I landed in a heap in the middle of the floor.

"Listen, punk," he growled under his breath. "You'd better watch your step. Something fishy has been going on around here, but I can't put my finger on it. When I do, you'd better look out."

So dear old dad was suspicious. Good! Let him try to figure out what I was up to. Monday I'd pick up another ton of stuff. He'd be so proud! In the meantime I sat down and emailed Chris and dumped on him as usual. Sure was glad I had someone I could pour out my feelings on. As usual I swore him to secrecy. He was not to tell his parents about what they were doing to me. Little did I know that he was showing them everything, saving everything, and printing everything. Doc had told him to.

Living in a fantasy world is great. I decided that when I let myself get caught I'd raise such a ruckus that it would hit every paper in the state. The first thing I'd tell the reporters was that Daddy Dear was considering running for Congress, but he didn't think he could afford it. So, I had done all of this to help him with his campaign fund. That would please him enormously. He thought that all politicians were a bunch of crooks. He always said that the last thing he'd ever do would be to run for some political office. If the truth were know, he probably realized that he couldn't get himself elected dog catcher with that charming personality of his.

Monday was a banner day. Walked into the camera shop to check things out and walked out with a five-hundred dollar digital camera. The one and only clerk in the store was feeding his face with a pecan roll and coffee and ignoring me. His mistake. Oh well, he'd get it back soon.

That afternoon I headed for the pool at Hunter Park. I was in such a good mood, I even waved at that lady with the screened in porch on Clifford St. Much to my surprise, she waved back.

The line at the pool wasn't too bad so I didn't have to wait too long. Deciding where to drop my towel, I spotted a mighty fine looking girl about my age filling out a rather scanty bikini and sitting all by herself. I spread out my towel about two feet away from her and plopped myself down and started slopping on the sun screen. It was time for me to make a friend. Hummmm! Before I could get totally situated, it got shady. Strange! I looked up and here was this huge character standing there talking to her. She was all giggles. He and all of his bulging muscles plopped down on the blanket with her. So much for that idea.

The way my luck was running I wouldn't meet one single, unattached girl my age until September when school started again. Here I had this beautiful tan straight from the sunny beaches of Florida, and there was no one around to appreciate. Rats! I opened my book and started to read.

Thursday morning found me browsing through the portable radios at Sears. Something wasn't quite right. That man a counter away looked familiar. Where had I seen him before? It didn't matter. I didn't want anyone around me who looked even vaguely familiar. Therefore, I wandered back to the sporting goods department. Checking out the sharpness of the fishing lures by weaving the barbs through the dead skin on my fingers, I spotted our man again taking practice swings with a golf club. It was time to get out of there. Fortunately, I hadn't lifted anything yet. I went into the snack bar and bought lunch—a bag of chips and a soft drink.

Hummmm! What was going on? There that character was again in line buying a cup of coffee. What a coincidence. Ha! He was following me and not being overly sneaky about it.

After I finished my nutritious lunch, I decided I might as well go home. It looked like I had struck out for the day. It was a good thing too because he followed me out the door. As soon as I was in the parking lot, he stopped me.

Hey, Kid. Just a minute," he said. "Mall Security." With that he flashed his badge for me to see.

"What do you want?" I asked shaking in my pants.

"I would like you to come to the manager's office with me, please."

"Why? I haven't done anything," I answered.

He didn't seem real impressed with my sincerity. As soon as we were inside, he ordered, "Empty your pockets on the desk and pull your shirt out from your pants and shake it out."

I did as I was told because I was clean. Fortunately, I had spotted him before I lifted anything.

My shirt was a very room men's size extra large of my dad's.

Since I wore a men's small, there was a ton of room in there to stash things.

"What is this, some kind of witch hunt?" I asked sarcastically. I was feeling a little braver since I knew he couldn't pin anything on me this time.

"Why are you in this mall every single day going from store to store? You never buy anything but food, yet you go through every single store. Why?"

"I like it here. I'm bored and I enjoy the air conditioning," I said a bit on the smart mouthed side. I couldn't believe my own ears the way I was talking. Maybe it was self preservation or something. Whatever it was, I wasn't overly proud of myself.

He kept me in there for over a half hour. He ended up by taking my name, address, telephone number, parent's name, and the works. He suggested very strongly that I stay out of The Shopping Center. I didn't know if he was just trying to scare me, whether he was bluffing, or what. I wasn't taking any chances, it was time to change my base of operations.

When I turned my bike into the driveway, I was surprised to see Dad's car there. I had gone to the pool straight from the mall because I didn't have anything to deposit in the attic. I knew it was a bit later than I normally got home; however, it couldn't be that late. He shouldn't have been home from work yet.

I found out the answer soon enough. Half way through the garage the fat man had me. He charged through the kitchen door into the garage like a raging bull. As a matter of fact, he kind of looked and smelled like one too.

He grabbed me by the arms by wrapping his pudgy hands around my biceps. He picked me up off the floor with both feet dangling in mid air and slammed me against the wall and screamed. Each time he bounced me off that wall. My head snapped back and smashed the wall too. He repeated it maybe five times. I tried to hold my neck rigid while he was doing it, but I couldn't. I thought sure my head would splatter against that wall like an egg. I wasn't thinking too clearly by the time he was done.

I do remember my mind screaming, "Explode, heart, explode!" I wanted to see him die right then and there in front of me. I never hated anybody or anything as badly as I did my dad.

Ole sweet and lovable Dad stopped gasping for air about a half hour later. His recovery time was getting longer and longer. One of these days that fat heart of his would blow up, and when it did, I'd spit in his face.

When he got his wind back enough to start screaming at me again, he told me I was never to go to The Shopping Center again by myself. That mall security agent had called him at work and told him of all his suspicions so fat boy came home early just for this very special occasion. That was the first I knew for sure why he had just beaten me up. He didn't say a word about my wearing his shirt. Probably saving that for the next session.

While I was in the bathroom cleaning up and washing down Tylanol for my head, he stomped out of the house with Mom in hot pursuit. What a pair! I had shamed them into another twelve pack or so to go along with their steak dinners. Hopefully, they left me something to eat. I knew that there was a can of hot dogs and beans in the cupboard. Didn't know what else. Had to investigate.

After my gourmet dinner, I picked up my cell phone and called Chris.

"What's going on?" Chris asked into the phone as he answered. He had Caller ID so he knew it was me. He had a worried tone to his voice.

"Had to hear a friendly voice," I retorted before I spent the next hour unloading my troubles on him. I told him a lot, but not everything. I told him what happened but not why. I guess I did quite a little ranting and raving about Dad.

"Ok, listen! Email me the specifics. I haven't told you this before but Dad has had me print off every one of your emails where you've talked about your dad abusing you. I don't know why he wants them. He just gets mad and swears under his breath every time I show him one. I don't know what he's doing with them, but I know he's keeping them."

"Ok, I will. Are they home tonight? I haven't talked to either of them for a while."

"No, it's their fifteenth anniversary. They've gone out to celebrate. They asked me to go, but I wasn't about to horn in on that. Mom cooked me dinner before they left so I'm in good shape."

After that we kind of caught up with each other. I hadn't talked to him in close to a week. Before we hung up, he bought up my problems with Dad again, "Nothing has changed between you and your dad has it?"

"Yes, there really has been a change," I answered truthfully. "I've grown to hate them both. Mom just follows that fat slob around as if everything is just great. Chris, I intentionally do things to antagonize him hoping to rile him up. He gets so mad at me that someday he's got to have a coronary, and I want to be the cause of it and see it happen. So help me, I'll spit in his face when he's checking out."

"Jason, that's a terrible thing to say. You don't mean it and you know it. You never talked that way before. I hate to hear you so bitter."

"Well, I am. I never knew what a home and a family and love was until I spent those seven months with you. Now I know what I've missed all my life, and I resent it. Sure I'm bitter. You would be too."

"Just hang in there. There has to be something Dad can do. He knows all kinds of important people. Make sure you Email me everything so he's got a record. Like I told you before, I don't know what he's doing, but hopefully he's got something in mind."

I sure as heck didn't know what he could do either, but it was a nice thought. If the truth were known, maybe Doc and Mona didn't really want to do anything. Maybe they were just as happy to be rid of the extra burden. I guess I demanded as much of their time, money, and attention as Chris did. If he needed help on his school work, so did I. If he got in trouble and needed to be talked to, so did I. If he needed shoes, so did I. We were like two peas in a pod. No wonder Doc used to say, "Here comes double trouble!" when we walked in together. They treated us like twins for all those months. God, I missed them all so much.

I never considered killing my dad, but forcing him into a heart attack was another matter. Maybe if I got caught stealing out of the stores, and they sent me to a juvenile home where he couldn't get his hands on me, the pressure would be so bad he'd burst an artery. It was worth a try.

Chapter Fourteen

The next two weeks were busy. I had to rip off enough so that it would be considered major by the courts, not just some petty kid's prank. Every day was a new adventure. One day I would go into downtown Lansing. Then I would hit the stores lined up and down Michigan Avenue from the capitol building to The Shopping Center about five miles to the east. After that I'd return to The Shopping Center. Dad forbade me to go out there, but what he didn't know didn't hurt him or me.

My stealing became more and more brazen. It finally got to the point where I'd walk into a store, pick up whatever I wanted, and walk out. For some reason or the other, nobody ever paid any attention to me.

The next week I received a long-long Email from Doc. Chris had told him everything that he knew. I felt guilty because he and Mona were worried about me. The Email was as much of a pep talk as anything else. He included a little lecture about my behaving myself. I laughed as I read it because all normal parents are alike. They can't help themselves when it comes to lecturing when the occasion calls for it.

The most important part was his private telephone number in

his office. He told me to write it down along with his cell phone number, his name, and address. He told me to label it as "In case of emergency," and put it in my wallet. If there was any trouble that I couldn't handle. I could give the information to anyone else and they could contact him for me. He reminded me that he was on my speed dial on my phone and that I hadn't called him lately and that he was sorry that he and Mona had missed my call when I talked to Chris.

How could I be doing such a stupid thing? Here I had people a thousand miles away who actually cared about me and were worried. Of course, that's the problem. A thousand miles is a long ways. Their Emails and phone calls helped and boosted my morale, but it wasn't the day to day relationship with their home and family that I really wanted.

A week and a half later I took inventory. I had a ton of valuables stashed in the attic. This was grand larceny at its best. I crawled up into my cache and made sure everything was in order. Today was the day.

Before I did anything with the cache, I boxed up my cell phone and mailed it back to Dr. Jackson. I wouldn't need it at the juvenile home. Then I went in and sat down on my computer and wrote the hardest Email that I had ever written. I sent it simultaneously to Doc, Mona, and Chris's email addresses.

I told them I was doing something horribly drastic, stupid, and intentional. I wouldn't tell them what I was up to because I was so ashamed of myself for doing it, but that I was putting myself into a position where I would be taken out of this lame existence and put away for good. I told them that nothing had ever really changed between me and my parents and I couldn't take it anymore. I was breaking off all communication with the Jacksons and walking out of their lives forever. I loved them all more than life itself and hoped that someday they would be able to forgive me. With tears dripping all over the key board, I hit send and turned off the computer.

It was time to do the deed. Dad was at work and Mom had gone to her bridge club. I dragged everything out of the attic down to the garage floor. Double checked all of the merchandise against my journal. Everything was accounted for. In the mean time the house phone rang continuously. Every time it went to voice mail, the caller hung up and hit redial. My best guess was Chris.

After wheeling into my favorite parking place at The Shopping Center, I started looking for my mall security guy. He probably still smiled every time he thought of the reaction he received from dear old Dad when he told him of his suspicions. He probably patted himself on the back every night when he thought about how he saved some kid from a life of crime. How little he really knew.

He wasn't anywhere in sight as I walked up and down the mall so I wandered over to Sears to check them out. No luck. Maybe he was on his coffee break. There were about a half dozen different places where he could be swilling coffee, but none of the worked out either. When I was just about ready to give up for the day, I spotted him standing next to a post reading a magazine. How phony! His eyes were looking right over the top of the magazine and staring holes through me. How he could ever catch anyone was a mystery to me. Nonchalantly, I meandered into the gift shop between us.

I didn't want him to miss a thing, so I went to the closest merchandise rack to the windows. There I grabbed a piece of junk jewelry and slipped it into my back pocket which faced the window.

The jewelry rack had little mirror like reflectors on it so I could see him pressing his nose against the window with his mouth open. He couldn't believe his eyes. He had finally caught me in the act. Hallelujah! It was his lucky day.

Whistling to myself to keep from laughing right out loud, I headed for the door. We met at the entrance.

"We meet again!" he proclaimed bursting at the seams.

"Hi," I said. "You just get to work? I've been looking all over this stupid shopping center for you."

"I just bet you have been. This time, though, you slipped up. I caught you in the act."

"Why, I don't know what you're talking about," I said as I poured on the pure, innocent little boy act.

"I'm going to have to ask you to empty your back pockets," he told me.

"And if I don't?"

"Then I'll just reach in your back pocket and take the chain you just stole out myself."

It was nasty, but I couldn't resist the temptation, "Look, if you want to put your hands in my pockets and cop a feel, this really isn't the place."

He flushed instantly, and I thought for a second he was going to smack me. I can't say as if I would have blamed him if he had.

"Don't be a little smart alec!" he growled at me. "I stood right there in front of that window and watched you pocket a gold colored chain. Now, are you going to take it out, or do you want to cause yourself even more trouble than you are all ready in?"

I reached into my pocket and pulled it out. "This cheap thing is really ugly, isn't it? So what are you going to do to me this time?" I asked handing him the chain.

"From here we go to my office and call your parents. They will have to come pick you up, and then you will be scheduled for an appearance at Probate Court.

"Why don't you just take me to the juvenile home and skip all the rest of that foolishness?" I asked.

"The only way I could have you just locked up right away would be if I knew you were an habitual offender and were a flight risk. I think you probably are, but I have no proof."

"If I can prove to you that I am, will you take me there before you notify my parents?

"Sure, but why? What's in it for you? You'd be better off having your parents going to bat for you."

"My old man is crazy, that's why. I lived in a foster home if Florida while he dried out for seven months and went through a child abuse rehab program. Well, it didn't work. The last time you called him he darned near killed me. He never even gave me a chance to explain, and I was actually innocent that time."

"Sorry to hear that. Really! He isn't going to be much of a help rehabilitating you then, is he?"

"None what so ever. That's why I've gone to all the trouble preparing for this. I want to be sent to the juvie jail or whatever they call it until I'm eighteen. They, when they kick me out of there, I'll just go in the service or something. One thing is for certain, I'm not going home again."

"You sound terribly bitter. Has it really been all that bad, or are you just having a rough spot right now. That does happen to a lot of kids, but things do eventually smooth over."

"Yes, it has been that bad and worse. Now, how about putting my bike in your car, and you can take me home so I can prove to you what a bad person I really am and that I need to be put away for a long time?"

"Do you think your parents can afford a lawyer, or don't you know that much about the family finances?"

"My old man is a lawyer, but I wouldn't use him. I don't need one anyway. I'll just plead guilty in front of the judge and get it over with."

"I'm afraid that Probate Court won't allow that," he laughed.

"A child advocate will be assigned to you and will work directly with your parents, the court, and everyone else making sure that whatever happens is in your best interest. However, I do give you credit for having a lot of spunk."

We dumped my bike in his trunk, and I told him how to get to our house. As we started down the street, I suddenly panicked. "Keep going," I said. "Go around the corner down there and stop. I've got to talk to you before we go back."

"What's the matter?" You act like you've seen a ghost!"

"I have, mine! My old man is in the garage looking at all the stuff I set out to show you."

"You really did set this all up with the idea of getting caught?"

"Sure. When I saw you peering over that magazine, I just slipped into the closest store and headed for the window. When I saw your reflection in the mirror, I slipped that piece of junk in my pocket. Here, this is good, pull over and stop for a minute. By the way, I'm sorry about that stupid comment about you putting your hand in my pocket. I was nervous and it just slipped out."

"Forget it!" he said with a smile. I think he knew that I was just spouting off at the time. Maybe a little false bravado?

I fished the card out of my wallet that I had written all of Dr. Jackson's numbers on and gave it to him. "This is contact information for my foster father in Florida. Would you be willing to call him some time tonight?"

"Sure. What do you want me to tell him?"

"Preferably not about the stealing unless you have to. He's a medical doctor and the first number is his office. If you call before five, you'll get his secretary, and she has been given orders to connect anyone who calls about me regardless of what he's doing. If you wait until after five, you'll get his answering service and you can just leave a message. That would probably be better anyway. That way you won't have to answer any questions. Rates are better too. Just tell him that I've been sent to the juvenile home, reform school, or where ever they send kids around here. Then tell him I'm sorry that I let them all down and ended up disgracing them. I know that my life is totally out of their hands now and that there is nothing they can do, but I feel an obligation to let them know what has happened to me. I emailed them kind of the same message, but I'd feel better if you let them know what's happened. Now, let's get back to my house so you can see what I've done and you can formally arrest me."

"Are you sure you want me to lay all that information on someone who is practically a stranger?"

"Stranger!" I gasped. "Doc, Mona, and Chris are the only people in the whole wide world that I ever loved. They took me and cared for me and loved me when my own family didn't. For seven months they were my mother, father, and brother. I love those people and it almost killed me to leave. They didn't want me to go either, but the stupid courts ordered it, and there was nothing anyone could do. Ever since Doc took me to the airport, my life has been miserable. The weird part is that in the eyes of the Probate Court, I was nothing but a foster child, but I know in my heart that they loved me too. My only hope is that they will remember that I used to be a good kid and won't hate me for what I've done."

When we pulled into the driveway, I could see the steam coming out of Dad's ears. While we were still walking towards the garage, he started screaming, "What is going on around here, as if I don't already know? Who's this guy, your fence?"

The security officer flashed his badge, "Ralph Yeomans, security patrol at The Shopping Center. I picked up Jason this afternoon for shoplifting. He told me he had a stash of stolen property here in the garage."

Totally ignoring the security officer Dad came after me, "I'm going to kill you! I'm going to leave you bloody and dead!" he screamed. He grabbed me by the throat with his left hand and started slamming his fist into my face. He broke my nose with the second blast. Blood started spurting all over the place. Mr. Yeomans grabbed him and tried to free me, but Dad's rage was just too powerful Mr. Yeomans finally bear hugged him at the same time Dad bear hugged me and charged at the garage wall using me as a battering ram. There was a homemade wooden coat rack hanging on the wall with two wooden shafts sticking straight out. He aimed me at that and we crashed into it using all of our combined weights to drive me. My mouth flew open in a scream and my eyes bulged as a searing pain exploded in my back. Everything started going black as the thoughts raced through my mind that he had turned the tables on me. He had killed me and would probably spit in my face.

Chapter Fifteen

I didn't hear the panic, the sirens, the ambulance, the screaming of my mother, the cursing of my father as the police drove off with him—nothing. I wasn't aware of them wheeling me into the operating room on my belly with that coat rack still sticking out of my back where it had wedged between the ribs. I didn't know that it was the bursting of my lung that caused the flashing lights in my head and the pain and blackness and not my heart exploding. I was out like a light.

Six hours of surgery and four more in recovery didn't leave me too cognizant of my surroundings either. The first thing I remember was the nurse holding my arm as she took my blood pressure.

"Welcome back to the world," she said smiling. "You've been out of it for a long time."

"I'm alive?" I answered. "I thought I was dying as the world went black."

"That's just nature's way. You passed out so you couldn't feel the pain anymore. You're going to be fine now."

I was lying on my belly and something very heavy was pressing down on my back. "What do you have on my back? It feels like it weighs a ton."

"Off hand, I'd say it might be close to an ounce of surgical bandages," she answered.

"That's all? They must be wrapped awfully tight."

"They aren't. It just seems that way. Don't worry. It'll start feeling better in the next day or two. Besides, all you feel is pressure. There is no pain. The doctors have made sure of that. In the mean time, now that you are awake and doing fine, they'll be taking you to your room in the pediatric ward. For the next couple of days you just take it easy and get a lot of rest. Right now, sleep is one of the best things you can do."

I must have dozed off after that because I don't remember anything until they moved me upstairs. Mary Marvin, the head night nurse, met our little entourage at the elevator.

"Hi, Jason. Welcome to kiddies' haven."

She chatted all the way down to my room smiling from ear to ear. Mary was a character. She was about five feet five inches tall and probably weighed a hundred and forty pounds. She had a touch of gray hair on her head and a ton of compassion in it. She was the perfect nurse.

She and the orderlies slid me onto the bed and situated my I.V. My back and chest were starting to throb all over. "The nurse downstairs told me that I wasn't going to hurt, but I am. I'm aching real bad," I told her.

"You just relax now, honey, and I'll be back in a couple of minutes with something for that pain."

I sure hoped so. I hurt all over! I hadn't noticed before Mary and the orderlies all left, but my mother was sitting in the chair in my room. She got up and came over to the bed. "How you doing, Son? You look pretty pale. Are you in a lot of pain?"

"It's not too bad, Mom," I lied. "Besides, the nurse said she was going to give me a pill or something. Where's Dad?"

"He's in police custody. I'll have to go pay his bail this

morning and get him out. They've arrested him for attempted murder. Isn't that something? That's really terrible. They'll never be able to make it stick. Sure, he got a little carried away, but he surely wasn't trying to kill you. Let's be honest here, you were not exactly doing the right thing yourself."

"Mom, when they release me from the hospital, I'm not going to go home ever again. I want to go to a juvenile home of some kind or reform school or someplace like that so Dad doesn't have an excuse to get "a little carried away" again. So don't let him get any fancy ideas about getting me off the hook. I broke the law and I'll pay the price." I couldn't believe it. She was actually sticking up for him.

"Let's not talk about it right now anyway. As soon as I get him out of there we'll come up to see you and start figuring out his defense. Somehow, you two are going to have to work together and help each other out of the scrapes you're in. I'm sure that between the two of you, you'll be able to come up with something."

"No way! I don't ever want to see him again. If he comes up here, I'll walk out. I won't talk to him, and I sure as the devil won't help him. As far as I'm concerned, he can rot in jail just like I'm going to. As long as we're not in the same place, I could care less."

"Oh, Jason, don't even think that way. I know you've been through a terrible shock, but just you wait, things will look differently in the morning."

"Mom, according to that clock, it's two o'clock in the morning, and I'm exhausted. Why don't you go home and get some sleep. You look awfully tired too."

"Okay, but I'll be back tomorrow sometime to see you."

"Mom, don't bother. You're going to be busy scraping up the bail money for Dad, and I don't want you to feel like you've got to hang around here. I'll be just fine."

"Don't be silly! I'll see you tomorrow."

She wasn't much more than out of the room and sleep came sneaking up on me again. The next thing I knew it was morning and they were sticking my breakfast tray on the cart beside my bed. I wasn't too hungry so I just picked at it. Finally someone came and took it away. I was so sore, I could hardly move.

As I was lying there feeling sorry for myself, another grandmotherly nurse came charging through the door pushing a cart. "Hi, Jason," she said. "My name is Betty and I'm going to be taking care of you in the daytime. If there is anything you need, just push that little button on that doodad pinned to your pillow. How are you feeling this morning?"

"Terrible! I hurt all over."

"Sorry about that, but what you're feeling is normal. I'll take care of it anyway. I'll just slip a little "feel better" juice into this little IV tube running into your arm, and you won't hurt anymore."

"Betty, I've got a favor to ask. I don't want my parents up here. Can you keep them out?"

"Your dad was the one responsible for this, wasn't he?"

"Yes! Is there any way you can keep him out of here? I don't think he'll come, but if he happens to, can you keep him out? I don't want to have anything to do with him ever again."

"I'll check with the doctor," she said. "We can close the door and put a 'No Visitors Allowed' sign on it if he okays it. That way we can screen your visitors, but it's pretty much impossible to deny access to your parents unless they see the sign and then just leave."

"That would be great for me and easy for you because you won't have anyone to screen. I won't have any visitors because I don't know a soul in this town other than my parents. I just moved here from Florida a little over two months ago."

"Ok, I'll see what I can do. In the meantime, let's see about getting rid of some of that pain. It will probably put you to sleep, but that's okay too. You need lots of rest right now."

I watched her as she put the medicine into the IV, and then she really surprised me.

"Before you go to sleep, we need to move you. Can't have you lying in one spot for too long. Don't want bed sores. Give me your right hand and pull."

Oh, did that ever hurt! My whole body throbbed. It hurt to lie on my back, but this rolling over thing was murder. She helped me on to my stomach to try for comfort purposes. That was worse than lying on my back. Next we tried lying on my left side and that wasn't too bad. That's the position I normally sleep on so she decided to let me stay that way for a while.

Thank God for that IV tube. For the next few days Betty and Mary would have turned my poor body into a pin cushion if it hadn't been for that. They were constantly putting in medication or drawing blood or something.

Betty hadn't much more than put in the shot and turned me on my side, and I was out. The next thing I remembered was the clanking of trays around my bed again. It was lunch time. Apparently, I was on no special diet, because I was served a decent lunch and I was hungry. The only thing I didn't touch was the prune juice. They had put it on my breakfast tray, and I hadn't drunk it then either. I couldn't stand the stuff.

After an orderly took the tray, Betty wandered in, "Hi, good looking," she said. "You feeling any better this afternoon?"

I hesitated a second or two before I answered because I thought she was making fun of my face which I was sure was totally black and blue. I know it sure felt like it was. Then I realized that she wasn't the type. She was just trying to be nice. "Betty," I answered, "You're too cheerful. I hurt, and I've got to go to the bathroom."

"Hey! You're pretty good! One out of three isn't too bad, Kiddo. If all the Detroit Tigers batted that well, we'd win the pennant every year."

"What are you talking about? What do you mean that one out of three isn't bad?" I asked confused knowing by the look on her face that she must be pulling my leg.

"Number one, a person can never be too cheerful. Would you want me to come in here all dejected and feeling sorry for myself? That would do your spirits a lot of good, wouldn't it?"

"At least we'd be soul mates on that score," I told her

She laughed and went on, "Number two. Of course you hurt. You wouldn't be here if you didn't. Your poor little body has been trashed. However, time and rest will take care of that, and you'll be out of here and as good as new before you know it."

"You really think there's hope that I'll feel like a human being again someday?" I asked.

"Yes, of course I do. Now quit interrupting because I'm only two thirds through lecture number 493. Number three," she continued with that smile on her face, "no, you don't have to go to the bathroom. You've had this little tube called a catheter in you since before you went into the operating room. It goes from your bladder to a little bag hooked on the side of your IV pole. But you don't have to worry about that, because that's one of the reasons I'm here all bright and early in the morning. I'm going to take it out of you."

I had no idea what Betty was talking about, but I soon found out. Modesty is not real high on the agenda in the pediatric ward. Betty pulled back the sheet and lifted my hospital gown. I had absolutely nothing on under it. Talking non-stop about nothing in particular, she proceeded to pull that little tube out of me. It embarrassed me something terrible, but she didn't seem to notice or care. It didn't bother her one bit. I guess she was more used to that sort of thing than I was.

If anything on this earth ever amounted to cruel and inhumane punishment, her next move did. "Okay," she said," hold on to my hand, and I'm going to help you sit up."

That in itself was horrible, but her next move was even worse.

"Okay, swing your feet over the bed. There you go, now, hold on tight and stand up."

"Betty," I protested. "What are you doing to me?"

"You and I are going for a walk," she answered very nonchalantly.

"Oh, no, we aren't! I can't walk! I can't even lie perfectly still without hurting. You can't make me do that."

"Jason, dear, I'll let you in on a little trade secret. As soon as you can walk to the nurse's station and back, you get to wear tightie whitie skivvies and cute pajamas with panda bears on them, and you also will have bathroom privileges. Until then, it's these darling, only slightly revealing, hospital gowns and bed pans."

"Let's go!" I said with an embarrassed grin.

I guess I never really knew the meaning of bribery until then. I thought I was going to die in the process, but I made it all the way to the nurse's station and back on the first try. True to her word, Betty bought me a pair of under pants and pajamas. They were awfully kiddish with their stupid panda bears all over them, but at least they weren't open in the back and that was all I cared about.

Mom showed up later that afternoon with the book I had just started along with a couple of sports magazines. She didn't have too much to say so, thankfully, she didn't stay too long. Dad's bond had been posted that morning so he was home working on his defense all ready. Being there seemed to make her nervous especially after I repeated what I had told her last night that I refused to ever go home again and did not want to see him ever again. My message must have sunk in because the next and last time I ever saw either one of them again was a few days later in Probate Court.

The reading material was welcomed because it gave me something to do besides watching television. I've never been one to watch a whole lot of it, and day time TV is strictly for the birds. I never could understand how anyone could watch the soap operas and game shows. They all seemed so stupid to me.

I wasn't supposed to get out of bed except to go to the bathroom. Since I still had an IV going, I had to call the nurse's station and one of them would come and help me. However, about four o'clock I was starved, and they said that dinner wouldn't be served until after five. So I managed to crawl out of bed and headed for the nurse's station dragging my IV stand.

"And just where do you think you're going, young man?"

Oops! Caught again. I turned around to see Betty standing behind me with her arms folded across her chest.

"Betty, I'm hungry! Do you nurses have anything stashed out here to tide me over until dinner?"

"Come on," she said with a smile on her face. I guess she wasn't too mad after all. "Let me pull the IV. You could trip over this rig and hurt yourself."

She took me down to the lounge and parked me at a table. Then she bought me some ice cream along with orders not to move until she came back to get me.

Other than getting rid of the IV, the next day was pretty uneventful. After that I could get up out of bed by myself and walk around all I wanted. Betty told me the more I walked the faster my body would repair itself. That night something weird happened. I wasn't sleeping real well and sensed that someone was standing by my bed. Someone was always checking on my day and night so I didn't think too much about it at first. Suddenly that person leaned down and kissed me on my cheek, stood up quickly, turned and headed for the door. By the time I woke up enough to open my eyes and focus, the person was headed out the door. It was a rather large man with a soft quiet walk. He gave me the impression of being a very gentle person as he moved. He moved just like Doc. I smiled to myself and fell back to sleep.

In the morning Mary Marvin was making her final rounds before getting off duty and I asked her about it. She smiled at me and pled ignorance of the whole thing. "Jason, let's just say you had a very pleasant dream. There really isn't any other explanation that I can give you right now."

There was something in her look that told me otherwise. She knew something that I didn't, but she wasn't talking.

I tried to pump Betty when she came on duty, but she had no idea what I was talking about either. For some reason or the other, I had the impression that both nurses were lying to me, and I couldn't understand why.

The day before I was released from the hospital, I had a visitor from Probate Court. Other than my mother's two visits, he was the only visitor I had the week I was in the hospital other than the surgeon and his staff and the various nurses who took care of me. He explained that he was some kind of referee that worked with the court and would be a type of liaison between the judge, my parents, and me. We talked for two hours and I laid it on the line, "I will not go to my parent's home to live. I've done something that was pretty bad and dishonest, and I only think it fair that they send me to the juvenile home until I am eighteen. Then I can be out on my own." I had it all figured out.

He was pretty evasive with any answers. He was more interested in hearing what I had to say than giving me any information. The only thing he said for sure was that I was scheduled to be released the next day at noon, and that he would pick me up. He did say that we would be going straight to Probate Court for a hearing that had been arranged. Other than that he wouldn't give me the time of day, much less what was going to happen to me.

Chapter Sixteen

One of my teachers told our class onetime that history had a tendency to repeat itself. When I walked into that hearing room the next day, I knew what he was talking about. The set up was almost exactly as it had been in Florida nine and a half months earlier. They had me sitting beside the official from Probate Court facing the judge's chair. My parents were on the other side of the room. The only thing that was different this time was that Doc was not sitting with me. Of course the circumstances were different this time too. The last time I was headed for the Jackson's to live. This time I was headed for the juvenile home.

When the judge entered, everyone rose. He shuffled his papers in front of himself for a minute or two and then turned towards me and spoke. "Jason, I've been on this bench for twenty years. In all that time I have never seen so many strings pulled, rules bent, and laws manipulated as I've seen in the past week. What makes this so unique and able to run so smoothly is that all the people involved with the decision that I am going to sign agree that it the right thing to do. Hopefully as you grow older, you will learn to appreciate what has been done this week in your behalf.

"Before I explain to you the decision of this court, I need to ask you some questions. I have been told certain things, but I want to hear them from you. First off, is it true that you do not wish to return to the home of your parents?"

"Yes, Sir," I answered softly. "That is correct."

"Do you understand that under normal circumstances because of your poor decisions and actions you could be placed in a juvenile institution until your nineteenth birthday?"

"Yes, Sir. Only I understood that it was the eighteenth."

"That pretty much depends on the dictates of the court. Of course, more than likely, much of that time would probably be in a foster home of some kind if you behaved yourself and didn't get into any more trouble."

"Yes, Sir. I understand.

"However, as I said, this has been a most unusual case right from the beginning. Four days ago a gentleman came to this court and asked if you, as a ward of the court, could be placed in his home as a permanent foster child.

"Who? Who was that?" I asked. Nobody in Michigan other than my parents even knew I existed, much less wanted me.

"Just hold on one more minute and let me finish," he told me. "I asked this person to give me twenty-four hours to check things out. Pouring over the law books, I discovered one little problem that wouldn't allow me to okay the transaction."

My heart sank. It sounded for a minute that I was going to get another chance, but apparently something was wrong.

The judge continued, "This man came back the next day with a plan. He had talked to the prosecuting attorney, your father and mother, their lawyer, all the people who filed charges against both you and your dad and came up with a proposal. Your dad and mother are losing their parental rights through all of this, but they still have to agree to what happens to you for the time being.

If your parents agreed to let you be adopted, the prosecuting attorney agreed to drop the attempted murder charges against your dad. With agreement signed, your surgeon and Mr. Yeomans from The Shopping Center both agreed to drop first degree child abuse charges against him. At the same time, Mr. Yeomans requested that all criminal charges be dropped from your record."

"Your honor, who is this person?" I was so confused by then, I didn't know what to think. Somebody was trying desperately to help me and I didn't even know who it was.

"One more question, and then I'll tell you," he said with a huge smile on his face. "Your name has been Jason Lee Anderson for almost twelve years. Do you think you could learn to get used to your name being Jason Lee Jackson?"

"Jackson? Doc? Oh, God, Judge. Where is he? Where's Doc?"

"I think you'll find that he has been sitting about ten feet behind you for the past fifteen minutes," he smiled. "Why don't you go say hello to him while I sign these papers?"

I turned around and there he was. We grabbed each other and held on for dear life. I couldn't even talk I was so shook up. He was breaking my back but I didn't care. I had Doc back.

When I finally pulled myself together emotionally so I could function again, I glanced over to the other side of the room. My birth parents were gone, out of my life forever.

A few minutes later the judge called the hearing back to order. He had to give me my lecture, "Dr. and Mrs. Jackson have shown a great deal of trust and love for you," he stated. "Dr. Jackson has spent a lot of time and money taking off work and flying here with the sole idea of making your life worthwhile and productive again. You had better appreciate it, and you must straighten yourself out. You have to avoid trouble at all costs. Don't ever make them sorry they did this. You have to promise me this much."

"Your honor, I promise before you, doc, and Almighty God that I'll never do anything to make them sorry."

"Okay," he said. "I have already agreed to this arrangement. However, there is one little catch that I put in to satisfy my own concerns. The final adoption does not go into effect until one year from today. Any time between now and then Doctor and/or Mrs. Jackson can change their minds. If they do, you will be returned to Michigan and once again will come to this hearing room. At that time we'll have to decide what to do with you. Incidentally, returning to your birth parents is not an option."

"Your honor, I promise, you'll never see me in this court room again."

"For everyone's sake, I hope not," he said as he signed and dated the papers he had in front of him. "You and Dr. Jackson are free to go now. Good luck to you both, and, Jason," he paused and then smiled, "try to be a good boy for a change."

"Yes, Sir!" I said smiling. Then I reached out for his out stretched hand and shook it.

When Doc and I left the courtroom, we jumped into his rented car and headed for the motel. We both talked practically non-stop all the way there. As soon as we were inside, he said to me, "Tonight we'll celebrate at the best restaurant we can find. But, right now, you're going to lie down and take a nap for a couple of hours."

"Take a nap?" I protested. "Why? I'm not a baby. I'm not even tired."

"In case you've forgotten over the past two and a half month's time, there are disadvantages to having a doctor for a dad. You had major surgery one week ago today. You were just released from the hospital at noon today, and right now you're all excited and keyed up. You will rest and take it easy for a couple of hours. I don't want that bicycle tire cement patch they put on your lung to pop off and start a slow leak. So, take off your clothes and jump right in under the covers. You don't have to sleep, but you are going to rest. Just shut your eyes and ignore me. I have some reading to catch up on and a couple of emails to send to my office so hopefully I won't disturb you."

I did as he said, except I didn't get under the covers. I threw the blankets back and just lay on the sheets. The air conditioner was going full blast and did it ever feel good. When I was snuggled in and comfortable, I looked up at him and said, "Ok, Doc, but I want you to know that I'm not the least bit sleepy." If Doc wanted to baby me just a little bit, that was fine with me. I'd rather be babied any day than beat on so I'd humor him and close my eyes and pretend to be resting.

"Hey!" doc said as he gently shook me awake. "For a guy who wasn't the least bit sleepy, this is getting ridiculous."

"Did I fall asleep?" I asked as I stretched, yawned, and then stretched again.

"Oh, of course not," he said grinning. "I think you were just resting your eyes. You lay down, shut your eyes, protested that you weren't at all sleepy, and haven't twitched a muscle in three hours. Now, I'm starved so get up, take your shower, and put on some clean clothes so we can go eat."

"Okay, but I don't have any of my clothes with me."

"Oh, I guess nobody thought to tell you, but I picked up all your clothes yesterday. Some are there in that suitcase and the rest have all ready been shipped to Florida."

True to his word, we went to the fanciest restaurant I've ever been to. He told me I could order anything on the menu I wanted so I had my first lobster. That was fun! The waitress put a big bib on me and then told me how to get at the meat. It was delicious!

During dinner we had a long, serious talk about how this came about. I didn't understand how he had found out so fast about my being in the hospital and in so much trouble.

"You were still in surgery," he told me, "When Bill Yeomans, the mall security officer, called me the first time. The only problem was, I was in the middle of an emergency and couldn't take the call. The receptionist answered the phone and let me know that somebody was calling about you long distance from Lansing. Obviously, I didn't recognize the name, so I asked if I could call him back later. He told her that he'd only be in his office for about another half hour, and that it was extremely important. As soon as I finished with my patient, I called him back.

"What did he say?"

"First off, he told me who he was and what his job was, and then he asked how well I knew you and how strong a relationship we had. He wasn't about to give out a lot of information to a stranger unless he was sure. When I told him about how you had lived with us for seven months, and that we hadn't wanted to send you back in the first place, he went ahead and told me what had happened."

"How much detail did he go into over the phone?"

"He talked for almost a half hour so I think he pretty much told me the whole story as he understood it. He said a lot of it he had learned for the first time that day himself. He told me about the shoplifting and what you had done with all the merchandise and all that. Then he told me that he had stopped you once before and that your dad had beaten the tar out of you. Of course, he hadn't known about that at the time. Then he told me how you set him up to catch you and that you had all the merchandise sitting on the garage floor. After that he told me about him taking you home and the trip around the block where you gave him my card and asked him to call me. When he took you home and your dad lit into you, it really shook him up. Your dad was in such a rage, there wasn't anything he could do to stop him. So, you see, he told me quite a lot about what happened right there on the phone."

"What all did he tell you about the trip around the block that we took before I let him take me home?"

"The most important thing, as far as I am concerned, was when you told him of your feelings for the three of us. You realize, I hope, that we all have the same feelings towards you. The only difference was, we had each other, and you didn't have anyone. You were stuck here all by yourself."

"And you have no idea how hard that has been. I've missed all of you so much!"I said kind of staring off into space. I continued, "So, I was in surgery when he called you. If that's the case, you didn't know if I were going to make it or not, did you?"

"No that's why I asked Mr. Yeomans if he would be willing to go back to the hospital and wait in the surgical lounge until the doctors came out so I could find out firsthand how you were. I told him to pretend he was somebody official if he had to, but it wasn't all that hard at all. Your dad was in jail, so your mom was waiting there by herself and appreciated the company. She recognized him from being at the house when the thing happened and just kind of assumed he was there in some kind of official capacity."

"How long did you have to wait?" I asked.

"Not really a long time at all. It was about two hours so I had plenty of time to call Mona and have her get me the first available flight out. She didn't like it one bit when I told her that she and Chris had to stay home, because I wanted to be able to move around quickly without always having to work around two other people. I guess Chris had a fit and fell in it when he found out he couldn't go. He wanted to come up here and punch out your dad personally. It was kind of funny at the time. Anyway, by the time Mr. Yeomans called back with the news, I had my flight number and the time so he volunteered to pick me up at the airport the next morning. He has been most helpful throughout this whole thing. Incidentally, he was very impressed with you."

"That's always good to hear. By the way, how did Mona and Chris take the news about my getting hurt and in surgery and all that?"

"I already told you Chris's reaction. He wanted to come up here and go after your dad. Mona went all to pieces over the phone. She started crying and calling your dad all kinds of names that I won't repeat. Then she got mad at me because I had let you go in the first place—as if I had anything to do with it. Then she'd cry again, I must say, she just had a wonderful time of it there all by herself with me listening in over the phone. At least she was able to get herself straightened out enough to get my plane reservations."

"When did you tell them about the stealing thing, and how did they react to that? Also, can we get my punishment out of the way now before we get home? I'm so excited about getting there; I don't want it hanging over my head. If I know what it's going to be, I can quit worrying about it."

"I told Mona about it right off over the phone. We didn't really get a chance to discuss it until I got home. Actually, everyone kind of discounted it as being unimportant. We figured it was just your way of crying out for help, and we were not there to give you any. We knew it wasn't the real you in action, so nobody gave it a second thought. Incidentally, Chris told us that was how the two of you survived when you ran away. He said that he was the one who had done all the stealing that time and that's probably what gave you the idea in the first place. So he tried to kind of take the blame for that part himself. So I guess you can just forget about any punishment and just concentrate on getting healthy."

"What happened here wasn't his fault or anyone else's. It was all my fault. I'm just glad it's over and that nobody hates me for doing it."

"No problem there. In fact, the entire episode brought out a side to Mona that I've never seen before. She can be a real bear when she wants to be. That night when we were packing my bag she kept telling me that I was going to have to bring you back somehow even if I had to kidnap you. She didn't care how I did it, just to make sure that I did. Knowing she was all riled up, I jokingly asked her, 'You really want me to bring that little thief home?' I've never seen her get so mad. I thought she was going to clobber me with something. She told me right then and there that she'd better not ever hear anyone refer to you as a thief even as a joke or she would rattle their brains."

"You mean she actually told you to bring me back when it first happened?"

"The whole situation was kind of funny really. She told me not to say anything to Chris, but that she wanted son number two home where he belonged. She didn't want to tell Chris anything about that possibility because of all the disappointment he'd feel if we couldn't pull it off. In the meantime, Chris kept pulling me aside telling me the same thing. 'Dad,' he said, 'bring my brother home. He's been gone way too long on this stupid little vacation away from us and I miss him. It's time he came home.' So you see, they were both telling me the same thing – bring Jason home where he belongs."

"I don't know what to say. I'm overwhelmed. My real family actually wants me back. When did you decide, Doc?"

"The first time I talked to Mr. Yeomans on the phone I knew I had to do something. I had to get you back home here where you belong. At first I figured it would probably be a foster home situation, but we could deal with that. We'd have you forever and that is all that mattered. The big question was how to pull it off without actually kidnapping you. Seriously, we couldn't have done that.

"Anyway, I went to your dad's office in the morning when I arrived in Lansing and he was already out on bond. Your mom was there so I got to talk to both of them. I told them at the time that I wanted to take you back to Florida for good. They actually agreed right away that it probably would be a good idea. They both said that they tried to make an effort to give you the home you deserve, but there were just too many issues that your dad couldn't overcome. They didn't go into a whole lot of detail, but I know the drinking and violence predilection had something to do with it. He's what some people call a mean drunk."

"So, tell me. How do Bill Yeomans and the surgeon both fit into all of this?"

"They were both filing 1st degree child abuse charges against your dad, and the prosecuting attorney was filing charges of attempted murder. The thing that really cinched everything for me was when your surgeon arranged for me to visit you without your knowledge in the middle of the night."

"That was you!" I said smiling. "I knew it was. I sensed it. All I got was a glance of you as you slipped out the door, but I just knew it was you. You kissed me on the cheek, didn't you?"

"Yes, I did. When I sneaked into your room and looked down at your battered nose, face and body, my heart almost broke right there on the spot. There you were on your left side with your left leg out straight and the right curled over the top of it. It was just like you were at home except for all the bruises and bandages. You looked so natural that I actually forgot where I was for a second. I grumbled at you under my breath asking you where the heck were your pajamas this time, and that you were going to catch pneumonia sleeping in your skivvies with no blanket. How many times had I seen your pajamas on the floor? How many times had I covered you up? How many times had you kicked the covers off as soon as I walked out the door? I was just about ready to cover you up when I realized what I was saying and shook my head. Then I said to myself, Jason, when I get you home, I promise, I'll never nag you about those darned pajamas and covering up again. I'll just turn up the heat."

"Progress!" I laughed. "I can't believe you didn't drag the covers up over me."

"I know, it's amazing. I just kissed you on the cheek and left."

Wow! Our feelings for each other were mutual. They wanted me as badly as I wanted them.

After we finally finished dinner we went back to the motel, and I went straight to bed. I still felt terribly weak and would for a long time. At seven the next morning Doc rolled me out of bed. We had a big day ahead of us. After breakfast we had an appointment at 9 A.M at the surgeon's office for a last minute check and change of bandages. He discussed the operation technicalities with Doc and told him what to keep an eye out for and what to do. He was to change the bandages every day for a week, and then they could come off for good. Doc was to take the stitches out about the same time depending on how things looked. The bandages were rubberized on the outside so I could take showers. Then came the restrictions.

"Jason, you know you were seriously injured, I don't have to re-hash all of that. However, I can't emphasize enough that you have to use good common sense and judgment. No swimming in the ocean until next summer. You can swim laps in a private chlorinated pool or lie on a float if it isn't crowded—but no horseplay. No contact sports probably for a year—I'll leave that up to your dad. I'm keeping you on antibiotics for a couple of weeks. I don't want you catching cold and sneezing or coughing. No getting caught outside in one of those famous Florida thunder storms."

Looked like my entire existence was going to be curtailed for a year. No football, baseball, wrestling, or anything that resembled a contact sport for the next school year. I had to take things easy for a long time. A punctured lung was nothing to mess around with.

Fortunately he said I could walk, jog, and ride my bike as I felt up to it. However, the bike was no big deal because the last I saw it, it was in Bill Yeoman's trunk. Who knows what ever happened to it. Who cared? Didn't matter. Probably my old man sold it for bail money. Whatever! When I was healthy again, I could mow lawns or something and earn some money and buy a new one.

Chapter Seventeen

By the time we finally left the surgeon's office, it was ten thirty. Doc took the prescription to the drug store and we picked up my antibiotics and some fresh bandages and medical supplies that he would need for me. We had some time to kill so he took me out to The Shopping Center where we found Mr. Yeomans and I had a chance to thank him and say goodbye. He really was a good guy. He wished me luck and a great life.

Then I showed him the pool at Hunter's Park where I spent my afternoons, and then we went to lunch. I was antsy and not very hungry and could hardly sit still. I kept looking at everyone who walked in suspiciously as if they were going to say that it was all a terrible mistake. Doc laughed at me and told me not to be so paranoid.

After lunch we went to Capital City International Airport there in Lansing and checked in his rental. There was a cafeteria where we parked ourselves while we were waiting to board the plane. I had a Coke and he ran off someplace to make a phone call where he could get better reception. I practically panicked when he left me alone, but fortunately, he wasn't gone long.

When he returned, he said, "Let's go. They called our flight about five minutes ago."

"I guess my mind was a million miles away, Doc. I didn't even hear them."

"Not a big surprise. Look around. This is probably the last time you'll ever be in Lansing. You're mine now, and I'm not letting you come back."

We both smiled and neither one of us said a thing—both absorbed in our own thoughts I guess. We went down the ramp to the plane and got on board, found our seats, and buckled ourselves in.

"Doc, two and a half months ago seems like centuries. When I got on the plane last time I was all alone and hurting badly. This time my heart isn't breaking."

"I know. All of our hearts were breaking too. This time we're together. Look out the window, we're almost down to the end of the taxi strip and ready to go on the runway."

"My stomach is doing flip flops like you wouldn't believe."

The pilot turned onto the runway and kicked that big bugger into over drive and we were rolling down the runway for takeoff. As the plane lifted off the runway, I relaxed. We were going home.

When we were airborne and the seat belt sign flashed off, I kicked off my shoes, curled my feet under me, and leaned back in the seat. Smiling down at me, Doc put his arm around me and pulled me close so I just rested my head on his shoulder for a second. The next thing I knew he was gently shaking me. My head was still on his shoulder.

"Gotta hook your seat belt back on and sit up. We're on the final approach to Tampa."

"What? We just left."

"About two and a half hours ago."

"Really? Wow! What a difference. When I went to Michigan, I popped those Dramamine you gave me the whole trip and was nervous as a cat. This time I sacked out the whole trip."

"Times have changed."

As we were walking towards the terminal, I asked Doc, "Is your car parked here at the terminal?"

"Nah! We're going to have to bum a ride from someone," he answered back.

Right then I saw them. Chris and Mona were standing by the gate. It had never dawned on me that when Doc made that call from Lansing he was calling Mona letting them know when we would arrive. Chris did not know until he saw me that I was coming. Mona had told him that they were trying to work something out but wouldn't know my fate until later.

We literally ran at each other, and I threw my arms around both of them at the same time. Mona gave me a big wet kiss right there in front of everyone, and I kissed her right back. We got a lot of smiles from people there in the terminal, and I was not the least bit embarrassed.

We grabbed our luggage and headed for home. What a reunion! All four of us talked a mile a minute. One almost had to take a number to get a word in edgewise. As we were approaching home, I asked Chris, "Did you ever change our room back to the way it was before?"

"Hey!" Chris Exclaimed. "I told you when you left that you'd be back. Of course I didn't change it."

Mona piped up, "The only thing that has been changed are your sheets. I did that this morning when I sent Chris to the store for something just to get him out of the house."

"I wondered why you sent me to the store for ice cream. We still had a gallon in the freezer."

We all laughed. It was great. I started to say something to Mona, and she stopped me in mid-sentence. "Jason, just a minute. Everything is all official and legal now. You are legally and emotionally my son. I've never liked to hear kids call their parents by their first names so I know I'd be more comfortable with you calling me Mom if that would be ok with you too."

"Get used to it? I'd love to. What about you, doc? Would you mind if I called you Dad? I'd rather do that than call you Doc."

"I can't think of a thing that would please me more. Besides it would sound a lot more intelligent than the Daaaoc thing you've been calling me the last two days."

Laughing, I explained to Chris and Mom, "I don't know how many times I started to call him Dad and then changed to Doc in the middle. I guess it did sound pretty stupid. I just didn't realize he noticed."

From that moment on they were Mom and Dad not only in name but in actions, emotions, and love. If I ever had to refer to the people who raised me the first eleven years, I would just call them the Andersons or those people in Michigan.

As we pulled into the driveway, Dad turned around in his seat and yelled at me pretending to be mad, "Jason, how many times have I told you not to park your bike in the driveway? One of these days I'm going to accidentally run over that thing!"

I couldn't believe it and neither could Chris. We all ended up laughing again for the umpteenth time since we had left the airport.

Dad had Overnight Expressed my bike and all my clothes the day before I was released from the hospital. Everything was shipped to the next door neighbor's house so Chris wouldn't know. When they left for the airport, the neighbor planted the bike in the driveway. Then the neighbor moved all of my clothes from his house to ours and put the boxes on my bed.

That afternoon after things settled down a little, Chris went to our room to unpack. When I started to put things away in my underwear and sock drawer, I stopped and pulled back. "Chris! What's this? There's a whole bunch of money in here."

"Oh, that's your allowance. Every week when Dad put mine on the top of the dresser, he would slip yours in the drawer. I told you that we all knew you were coming back. We just didn't know when."

"I can't take that!"

"You know you can't argue with Dad about stuff like that. We'll just go down to the credit union and open you up a savings account just like I have. It will come in handy one of these days. You might need a new IPod or something and you'll have the money."

All I could say was, "Wow!"

Chapter Eighteen

The next few days were pretty busy. School was going to be starting within the next two weeks. Friday morning Mom told me, "Jason, don't make any plans for tomorrow. We're going shopping."

"What for?" I asked

"School clothes. We're late getting this done. I just hope everything isn't too picked over."

"Mom, I don't need any new clothes. All the stuff you bought me last spring is still good and still fits. No sense wasting a bunch of money on new clothes when I don't really need them. I'll be fine."

Mom gave me that look and replied, "Jason, don't make any plans for tomorrow. We're going shopping."

Chris snorted and I just smiled and answered, "Yes, Mom."

The next morning she rousted me out of bed around seven thirty and said, "Get up lazy bones. Times a wasting, we're headed out to breakfast before the stores open."

And we did. We both had blueberry pancakes, hot syrup, and crisp bacon. First time I ever had blueberry pancakes. "This ought to help put a little of the weight back on that I lost while I was gone," I told her.

Mom started laughing, "It's not really funny, but I've only seen your dad go totally ballistic maybe five times in the fourteen years we've been married, and two of them evolved around you. The first time was when he called me after he saw you in the hospital in the middle of the night, and the other was during your September 1st weigh in when he saw that you had lost five pounds while in Michigan."

"He did kinda go on a rant about how anyone could with hold food from a child, didn't he? What did he say when he called you after he came to the hospital?"

"I didn't know what was going on. It must have been one o'clock in the morning when he called ranting and raving about Bill Anderson and what he had done to you. It took me a minute to wake up, get oriented, and figure out what he was swearing about. Needless to say, I didn't get any more sleep that night."

"I'm sorry."

"Not your fault, Sweetie, it was that jerk who caused all the problems, not you.

"I know, but you know what? Everything he did was worth it just to have my life like it is now."

"You have no idea how many times Dad and I have talked about this. There is no way in the whole wide world that we would have ever wanted you to go through what you did. Yet, if you hadn't, we wouldn't have you now. I don't want you to take this wrong, but I'm glad it happened."

"I know. I feel the same way."

The rest of the day went great. It was just Mom and me being together and shopping and talking and hanging out together. I didn't care so much about the new clothes as I did with the one on one time with her.

As time went on I noticed that just about once a week I ended up with either Mom or Dad for some kind of outing for a good part of the day. One time I was with Mom and Chris was with Dad, and the next time it was reversed. My life had certainly changed.

After Christmas and before New Year's we had just sat down for dinner when Dad became very serious. "Boys, I have something to discuss with you. I want you to just eat your dinners and listen to what I have to say and don't interrupt."

Chris and I looked at each other and both of us had that look. 'Oh, oh! What'd we do this time?'

"When Grandma and Grandpa Jackson went back to Texas after visiting during Thanksgiving, he emailed me this picture. "

Chris saw it first and said, "Where did you get that ugly shirt? I haven't seen you wear that thing before."

"Let me see," I said. "I don't remember having that picture taken." I said after taking a look. "That has to be some kind of Photo Shop creation. I agree with Chris. I wouldn't wear a shirt that looked like that."

Mom and Dad were both smiling as Mom said, "To start with, the picture is not a Photo Shop creation. That's your dad on his thirteenth birthday."

"Whoa! Let me see that again," I said as Chris jumped up and ran around the table to take another look with me.

I couldn't believe it. When you took a real good look at the picture, you could see that it was Dad, but it sure looked like me.

"Ok, story time," Dad started. "When I was in my last year of medical school, Mom and I were married and horribly broke. I had no money to get her a Christmas present. I was talking to one of my professors and he suggested the fertility clinic in Miami as they would pay for donations if you qualified. I did. I bought Mom a pair of gold ear rings for Christmas."

"Right! I know! The ones she always wears. The ones she has on now," Chris stated.

"I told Mom about it after Christmas and we always wondered if there was another little Jack Jackson running around out there someplace. But, you know, time goes on and you kind of forget those things.

"Then you came on the scene and you kind of resembled me, and Mom and I have even joked about it. We even talked about how the four of us bonded so quickly and easily as being somewhat eerie.

"We've also talked about how Chris always insisted he had a brother out there someplace—that he sensed it. Yet he never knew a thing about the story behind the ear rings.

"When Grandpa sent that picture, in the subject line he put, 'No embarrassing questions, but get a DNA test on Jason.' Above the picture he wrote, 'According to the world famous philosopher, Playdough, there ain't no such thing as a coincidence.' You know, Grandpa does have kind of a weird sense of humor."

So Mom and I talked about it and decided to do just as Grandpa suggested. Do you remember when you came in for your flu shots around the first of December how the nurse took a swab of the inside of your cheeks?"

"I thought that was pretty weird, but when I asked the nurse, she just said, 'Oh, that's just your dad leaving no stone unturned. You know how he is,'" Chris said.

"Anyway, Jason mentioned on a couple of occasions that Bill Anderson screamed at him several times when he was mad at him that he wasn't his kid. I called Mary Anderson and asked her if there was any truth to it. I told her I needed to know for Jason's medical records. She told me that it was true. She had visited a fertility clinic in Miami in December thirteen years ago. They were having marital troubles at the time and thought that maybe having a baby would bring them all together. It didn't work. Bill couldn't handle it. He always said that if God had wanted them to have kids, He would have given them one of their own. He could not accept Jason as his own son.

"Before she hung up, she said, 'Oh, by the way. The donor at the fertility clinic was supposed to be a young doctor. Have you ever noticed how much Jason looks like you? Hummmm! Let me know if you ever find anything out for sure.'

"The results came back yesterday. You two are close enough genetically to pass as fraternal twins. And, yes, Jason, just for the record, you ARE that other little Jack Jackson running around out there."

Chris and I looked at each other and started laughing. We keyed off of each other all the time.

"And what is so funny?" Dad asked.

"Dad, Jason and I have known this forever. We just didn't know the details. How it actually happened we hadn't figured out. I really don't want to say what all our theories were."

"Probably just as well you don't," Dad said with a little smirk on his face. I think he was getting a kick out of this.

"Jason and I have been passing ourselves off as fraternal twins for two years now."

"And how did you get around the fact that your birthdays are two weeks apart?" Mom asked with a smile.

"Simple, we just told everyone that I was born a week early."

"Which, Of course, you were," Mom added.

"And Jason was born a week late," Chris continued, "And he was. And then, to top it off, we just told everyone that somebody around here refused to get a caesarian so our birthdays could be on the same day."

"So now your birthdays being two weeks apart is all my fault?" Mom asked with a wide eyed look of disbelief.

Chris and I looked at each other, raised our eyebrows, gave

each other a goofy look, and shrugged our shoulders. Then all four of us laughed.

My head was exploding. I didn't know what to say. Chris and I had joked about this for a long time. He swore it was all true—he sensed it. It was very important to him. I just always loved the idea as a wonderful coincidence and wishful thinking. Whatever! It didn't really matter anymore. The only thing that was important was that I was where I was loved and wanted. I was home.

The End

Also available from PublishAmerica

NOW THAT I KNOW
by P.J. Christian

Now That I Know is a love story that leads to tragedy to the point of suicide. It is about a girl who suffers great pain from making a life-altering, destructive decision to have an abortion and the downward spiral that follows. She aches and spends many days stuck in anxiety, wishing she could undo what she did, because she *now knows*. She tries many ways to compensate for the despair, but this only leads to more sorrow to the point she believes life is not worth living. In her darkest moment with the intention, method, and suicidal plan, all is lost, and dying would be the only way to ease the pain. In that instant someone loves her enough to reach out, pull her out of the depths of hell, and give peace, new meaning, and purpose to her life.

Paperback, 110 pages
5.5" x 8.5"
ISBN 1-60441-570-3

About the author:

P.J. Christian has written sports articles for newspapers and two articles about her experience as a traveling nurse. Inspired by God to write this book about this very dark, hidden secret of her past, she writes to share how God can take a broken, worthless life and transform it. Now that she knows about abortion and the life-changing reality of Jesus Christ, she offers that knowledge to you.

Available to all bookstores nationwide.
www.publishamerica.com

THE DAY SATAN REPENTED
by Cicero Ernest Curry II

Imagine growing up in the Bellows family where an eternal curse has been placed on them throughout the generations by a witch doctor. With each succeeding generation, only one male could be born within their family unit. The wives of these men could not give birth to any females because the witch doctor caught her husband in bed with his mistress.

These men have been watched throughout the ages by Satan who has in fact designed this curse for his eventual return to walk upon the earth. Known as Lokanetra, he is disguised at first as a great miracle healer. Then, as his fame grows, he brings together the leaders of the Middle East, ending the raging conflicts that have ravaged the region. Through Satan's final act of deceit, his main objective is to have a son born by way of his spirit-filled seed with a virgin wife.

Paperback, 128 pages
5.5" x 8.5"
ISBN 1-60474-692-0

About the author:

I am a sixty-two-year-old writer who can remember being a twenty-three-year-old who had a dream of writing a novel someday. I am socially active living in the beautiful city of Portland, Oregon. I have been married for thirty-three years and I have eight children and five grandchildren.

RECOGNIZING SATAN
by Audrey Kenner

Many troubles we face in life have some explanation; we can attribute them to bad behavior, past experiences, trauma, mental illness, even insanity. But what about when such explanations fail? What of a loved one changing inexplicably into a different person altogether? And what is it when someone who barely knows us deliberately targets us to unleash his ill will?

AUDREY KENNER
RECOGNIZING SATAN

A CASE FOR EXORCISM IN MODERN TIMES

Paperback, 253 pages
6" x 9"
ISBN 1-4241-9599-3

One explanation is demonic force. One solution that's lost its popularity is exorcism. Throughout history and even today, demons have inhabited human bodies to do evil. Satan exists today, challenging our faith, hoping that we're ignorant of the awesome power of Christ. *Recognizing Satan* exposes how the devil operates in the lives of both sinner and saint.

About the author:

Audrey Kenner was born in Chicago, Illinois. She met her husband Brian at sixteen. Brian felt the call to the ministry two years later and was ordained; they married one year thereafter. Audrey attended Columbia College (Chicago). They have been married for twenty-seven years and they have two children and three granddaughters.

Also available from PublishAmerica

SEPHARDIC FAREWELL
by Joseph Hobesh

Late fifteenth-century Spain, Queen Isabella
and King Ferdinand issue the Expulsion Edict.
Non-Catholics have two choices: convert to
Catholicism, or leave Spain with nothing. The
monarchs provide Columbus funds for his first
exploratory sea voyage. Against the historic
sweep of Columbus' voyage, the expulsion of
the Jews, and the exploration of the New
World, one family chooses to remain in Spain,
living as Catholics, while another emigrates
to Turkey to continue their Jewish faith.

Uprooted by the edict, the Halavi family is
dispersed. Joshua Ben Halavi sets sail with
Columbus, while Benjamin and his father,
David, settle in Constantinople, establishing
deep Jewish roots.

Paperback, 247 pages
6" x 9"
ISBN 1-4241-6247-5

The San Miguels, whose Jewish roots have
been well-hidden for many years, choose to remain in Spain as Christians,
their fate a mixture of Inquisition horror and New World success. From the
historic voyage of Columbus and the colonization of the Americas,
Sephardic Farewell follows these two families, portraying their lives
through the sweeping events of the fifteenth and sixteenth centuries.

About the author:

Born and raised in New York City on the Lower East Side,
Joseph Hobesh worked as an electrical engineer until 1996
and is now retired. Being of Sephardic ancestry, the subject
of the Jews' expulsion from Spain has always held immense
interest for Joseph, and he has been working on this project
since 2002. Married with five children, including a set of
twins, Joseph resides in Lafayette, California, with his wife,
Anita, where in addition to writing, he is an avid senior softball player, and
grandfather.

Available to all bookstores nationwide.
www.publishamerica.com